Agatha Christie

The Body in the Library

Collins

Collins

HarperCollins Publishers
The News Building
1 London Bridge Street
London SE1 9GF

www.collinselt.com

This *Collins English Readers* edition first published by HarperCollins Publishers 2017.

10 9 8 7 6 5 4 3 2 1

First published in Great Britain by Collins 1942

www.agathachristie.com

ISBN: 978-0-00-824969-4

A catalogue record for this book is available from the British Library.

Cover design © HarperCollins*Publishers* Ltd/Agatha Christie Ltd 2017

Typeset by Davidson Publishing Solutions, Glasgow

Printed and bound by CPI Group (UK) Ltd., Croydon, CR0 4YY

Contents

◆ INTRODUCTION ◆

ABOUT COLLINS ENGLISH READERS

Collins English Readers have been created for readers worldwide whose first language is not English. The stories are carefully graded to ensure that you, the reader, will both enjoy and benefit from your reading experience.

Words which are above the required reading level are underlined the first time they appear in a story. All underlined words are defined in the **Glossary** at the back of the book. Books at levels 1 and 2 take their definitions from the *Collins COBUILD Essential English Dictionary*, and books at levels 3 and above from the *Collins COBUILD Advanced English Dictionary*. Where appropriate, definitions are simplified for level and context.

Alongside the glossary, a **Character list** is provided to help the reader identify who is who, and how they are connected to each other. **Cultural notes** explain historical, cultural and other references. **Maps and diagrams** are provided where appropriate. A **downloadable recording** is also available of the full story. To access the audio, go to www.collinselt.com/eltreadersaudio. The password is the tenth word on page 5 of this book.

To support both teachers and learners, additional materials are available online at www.collinselt.com/readers. These include a **Plot synopsis** and **classroom activities** (both for teachers), **Student activities**, a **level checker** and much more.

ABOUT AGATHA CHRISTIE

Agatha Christie

Agatha Christie (1890–1976) is known throughout the world as the Queen of Crime. She is the most widely published and translated author of all time and in any language; only the Bible and Shakespeare have sold more copies.

Agatha Christie's first novel was published in 1920. It featured Hercule Poirot, the Belgian detective who has become the most popular detective in crime fiction since Sherlock Holmes.

Collins has published Agatha Christie since 1926.

THE GRADING SCHEME

The Collins COBUILD Grading Scheme has been created using the most up-to-date language usage information available today. Each level is guided by a comprehensive grammar and vocabulary framework, ensuring that the series will perfectly match readers' abilities.

		CEF band	Pages	Word count	Headwords
Level 1	elementary	A2	64	5,000–8,000	approx. 700
Level 2	pre-intermediate	A2–B1	80	8,000–11,000	approx. 900
Level 3	intermediate	B1	96	11,000–20,000	approx. 1,300
Level 4	upper-intermediate	B2	112-128	15,000–26,000	approx. 1,700
Level 5	upper-intermediate+	B2+	128+	22,000–30,000	approx. 2,200
Level 6	advanced	C1	144+	28,000+	2,500+
Level 7	advanced+	C2	160+	*varied*	*varied*

For more information on the Collins COBUILD Grading Scheme go to www.collinselt.com/readers/gradingscheme.

CHAPTER I

In her sleep Mrs Dolly Bantry <u>frowned</u>. Something was waking her – someone was coming – too quickly and too early. This was not Mary bringing the morning cup of tea.

A knock came at the door. Without properly waking up, Mrs Bantry said: 'Come in.' The door opened and Mary's frightened voice said: 'Oh, Mrs Bantry, Mrs Bantry, *there's a body in the <u>library</u>.*'

And then she ran out again in tears.

Mrs Bantry sat up and shook her husband.

'Arthur, Arthur! Wake up!'

<u>Colonel</u> Bantry[1] <u>grunted</u> but he didn't wake up.

'Arthur! Did you hear what Mary said? There's a body in the library!'

'You've been dreaming, Dolly,' he said. 'It's that detective story you were reading where a beautiful blonde woman is found dead on the library rug. Bodies are always found in libraries in those stories. It doesn't happen in real life.'

'Arthur, you've got to get up and see.'

'But Dolly, it *must* have been a dream.'

Mrs Bantry jumped out of bed and pulled open the curtains.

'I did *not* dream it, Arthur! Go and see about it.'

Colonel Bantry grunted again but put on his <u>dressing gown</u> and left the room. The servants[2] were all standing together at the bottom of the stairs, looking worried. Lorrimer, the butler[2], stepped forward.

'I said that we shouldn't do anything until you came, sir. Shall I ring the police now?'

'About what?'

The butler glanced at Mary, who was crying on the cook's shoulder.

'I understood, sir, that Mary had told you. She went into the library – and almost fell over the body.'

'Do you mean to tell me,' demanded Colonel Bantry, 'that there *is* a dead body in my library?'

Miss Jane Marple's telephone rang when she was dressing.

'Dear me, I wonder who that is?'

Neighbours in the village[3] of St Mary Mead called each other between nine o'clock and nine-thirty in the morning to make plans for the day, but it was now only a quarter to eight.

'It must be a wrong number,' thought Miss Marple.

She answered the phone. 'Yes?'

'Is that you, Jane?' Mrs Bantry sounded excited. 'The most awful thing has happened. We've found a body in the library.'

'A *what?*'

'I know. I thought they only happened in books.'

'But whose body is it?'

'It's a blonde girl – lying in the library, dead, so I'm sending the car to get you – you're so good at murders. She's been <u>strangled</u>, you see. And if I've got to have a murder in my house, I suppose I'll have to try and enjoy it. That's why I want you to come and help me find out who did it. It *is* rather exciting! I know it's very sad, but I don't know the girl – and she doesn't look *real*. You'll understand what I mean when you see her.'

When they arrived at Gossington Hall[2], the driver held the door open and Miss Marple got out of the Bantrys' car.

Colonel Bantry came out onto the front steps, looking a little surprised.

'Miss Marple? – er – I'm very pleased to see you.'

'Your wife called,' explained Miss Marple.

'Good. She should have someone with her. It's been a shock.'

At this moment Mrs Bantry appeared. 'Go back into the dining room and eat your breakfast, Arthur,' she said.

Her husband did as he was told.

Mrs Bantry turned happily to Miss Marple.

'*Now!* Come on.'

She led the way to the library door where the village policeman, Palk, was <u>standing guard</u>.

'I'm afraid nobody is allowed in, ladies,' he said.

'Oh, Palk. You know Miss Marple, and it's very important that she sees the body,' replied Mrs Bantry.

Constable Palk[4] <u>gave in</u>. He always gave in.

'Don't touch anything,' he warned.

'Of course not,' said Mrs Bantry. 'We know *that*.'

Mrs Bantry led her friend to the middle of the room and pointed <u>dramatically</u>.

'There!'

The library was large with one or two good family <u>portraits</u> on the walls, and some other low quality paintings. It was a <u>well-used</u> room, with a feeling of history to it.

And lying across the old rug was something new and <u>crude</u> that did not fit the room – a girl with fashionably curly, <u>dyed</u> blonde hair. Her thin body was dressed in a cheap evening dress of white silk with <u>sparkles</u>. She wore lots of make-up on her <u>swollen</u> face. Her lips and her <u>fingernails</u> were painted blood red. Miss Marple understood what her friend had meant when she said the dead girl didn't look real.

Miss Marple said in a gentle voice: 'She's very young.'

She <u>bent down</u>. The girl's fingers were <u>gripping</u> the front of her dress – she had pulled at it in her last horrible fight for breath.

There was the sound of a car outside. Constable Palk said urgently: 'It's Inspector Slack[4]...'

Mrs Bantry immediately moved to the door and Miss Marple followed her.

Colonel Bantry was pleased to see Colonel Melchett, the Chief Constable[4], getting out of the car with Inspector Slack. He had never liked Slack – he was a man who didn't care about the feelings of anyone he didn't think was important. But Melchett was Bantry's friend.

'Morning, Bantry,' said Melchett. 'I thought I should come along myself. Do you know who the woman is?'

'No, no idea!'

'Right,' said the Chief Constable. 'I hope your wife isn't too upset, Bantry?'

'No, she's been wonderful. She's got Miss Marple with her – from the village. A woman wants another woman when something important happens, don't you think?'

Colonel Melchett laughed: 'If you ask me, your wife's going to try a little <u>amateur</u> detective work. Miss Marple's quite famous for it around here!'

In the dining room, Mrs Bantry said: 'Well, Jane? Doesn't it *remind* you of anything?'

Miss Marple was famous for her ability to connect simple events that happened in the village with more serious problems. Then the serious problems could be seen more clearly.

'No, I can't say it does,' she replied. 'I was reminded a little of Mrs Chetty's youngest child, Edie, but I think that was just because this poor girl bit her nails and her front teeth <u>stuck out</u> a little. And, of course, her dress. Very bad quality.'

'But what could she possibly be doing in our library? Palk told me that the window was broken. Maybe she came here with a <u>burglar</u> and then they argued?'

'She wasn't exactly dressed for that,' said Miss Marple.

'No, she was dressed for dancing or a party. But there's nothing like that around here.'

'Well…' said Miss Marple.

'What, Jane?' asked Mrs Bantry.

'Basil Blake.'

Mrs Bantry cried: 'Oh, no! I know his mother – she's the nicest woman.'

'I'm sure she is, but there has been a lot of *talk* about Basil.'

'Oh, I know. And he was *very* rude to Arthur recently, and now Arthur won't hear a good word about him. And the *clothes* he wears! Oh, but he was the sweetest baby…'

'There was a lovely picture of the Cheviot murderer as a baby in the paper last Sunday,' said Miss Marple.

'Jane! You don't think *he—*'

'No, no, I didn't mean that at all. I was just trying to find a reason why that young woman was here. Basil *does* have parties. People come from London to them, you know, and recently there's been a young woman with him – a blonde.'

'You don't think it's *this* one?'

'Well, I've only seen her getting in and out of the car, I've never seen her face and all these girls with their make-up and their hair look so alike.'

'Yes. So, it *might* be her. It's an idea, Jane.'

CHAPTER 2

A different idea was being discussed by Colonel Melchett and Colonel Bantry at that same moment.

'Listen, Bantry,' said Melchett. 'If you *did* have a relationship with this girl, you must tell me about it *now*. I'm not saying *you* strangled the girl – it's not the sort of thing you would do, I *know* that.'

'Honestly, Melchett, I've never seen that girl before in my life!' said Bantry.

'All right. But what was she doing in your library? She *came* here, so she must have wanted to see you. Have you had any strange letters?'

'No, I haven't.'

'What were you doing last night?'

'I went to a meeting,' replied Bantry. 'I left just after ten o'clock and had to stop on the way home to change a tyre on the car. I got back here at a quarter to twelve.'

'You didn't go into the library?'

'No. I went straight to bed.'

'What about your wife?'

'She was already in bed asleep.'

'It's possible that one of the servants may be involved...'

Colonel Bantry shook his head.

'I don't think so. They're all very honest. They've worked here for years.'

'Well then,' said Colonel Melchett, 'it's likely that the girl came here from London, perhaps with a young man. Though I don't understand why they wanted to break into this house—'

Bantry interrupted.

'Oh, Basil Blake! A nasty young man who works in the film industry. He's living in a cottage on Lansham Road. He has noisy parties there and girls often visit for the weekend. There was a girl here last week – one of these dyed blondes—'

Bantry stopped.

'Melchett, you don't think—'

'It's a possibility,' said the Chief Constable. 'Inspector Slack and I will go and have a chat with Basil Blake.'

Basil Blake's cottage was just outside the village.

The local people had been very excited when they heard the news that a film star had bought the house. Then they learned the true facts. Basil Blake wasn't a star – he wasn't even a film actor. He was a very low-level <u>set decorator</u> for Lemville Studios, and the village girls were very disappointed.

Colonel Melchett knocked on the front door. It was opened by a young man with long black hair, wearing orange trousers who said angrily: 'What do you want?'

'Are you Mr Basil Blake? I would like to ask you a few questions, please. I'm Colonel Melchett, Chief Constable.'

Blake said rudely: 'How interesting! And?'

Trying to speak pleasantly, Colonel Melchett said, 'You're up early, Mr Blake.'

'I haven't been to bed yet. What do you want to speak to me about?'

'I've been told that last weekend you had a visitor – a – er – blonde-haired young lady.'

Blake laughed loudly.

'Have the old cats from the village complained to you? <u>Morals</u> are nothing to do with the police.'

'No, I'm here because the body of a young blonde woman has been found – murdered. In the library at Gossington Hall.'

'At Bantry's? And you've come to ask *me* if I'm missing a blonde?'

A car arrived with a noisy sound behind Melchett. A young woman with blood red lips and bright blonde hair got out. She said angrily to Blake: 'Why did you leave me?'

'I told you that we should leave and you wouldn't.'

'I was enjoying myself. If you think you can tell me what to do, you can think again!'

Colonel Melchett coughed politely.

'This is Dinah Lee,' Basil Blake said. '*My* blonde, who is alive and well. Now perhaps you'll <u>get on with</u> finding out what happened to old Bantry's blonde. Goodbye!'

CHAPTER 3

In his office, Colonel Melchett was listening to Inspector Slack:

'… so it all seems clear, sir – Mrs Bantry went to bed just before ten. The servants went to bed at half past ten and Lorrimer, the butler, at a quarter to eleven. Nobody heard anything.'

'What about the broken window?'

'It wouldn't have made much noise.'

The door opened and Dr Haydock, the police doctor, came in.

'I thought I'd tell you my first ideas before I do a complete examination. The girl was strangled with the belt of her own dress. The murderer didn't have to be strong – I think he or she surprised the girl.'

'What was the time of death?'

'Not earlier than ten and not later than midnight. She was young – only about seventeen or eighteen.'

The doctor left the room and Slack said: 'Colonel and Mrs Bantry *must* know something. I know they're your friends, sir, but—'

Melchett gave him a cold look.

'Slack, I'm considering *every* possibility. Have you looked through the list of people who have been reported missing?'

Slack showed him a typed sheet of paper.

'Mrs Saunders, reported missing a week ago, dark hair, blue eyes, thirty-six years old.

'Mrs Barnard, sixty-five.

'Pamela Reeves, sixteen, went missing last night, had been at a meeting of the Girl Guides, dark brown hair—'

'You don't need to read all the stupid details, Slack. This wasn't a schoolgirl. In my—'

He paused when the telephone rang. 'Hello – yes – what? Just a minute—'

He listened, and wrote quickly. Then he spoke again:

'Ruby Keene, eighteen, professional dancer, five feet four inches tall, thin, blonde hair, blue eyes, believed to be wearing a white evening dress and silver sandals. What? Yes, there's no doubt about it. I'll send Slack over immediately.'

He put the phone down and looked at Inspector Slack. 'That was the Glenshire Police.' (Glenshire was the next <u>county</u>.) 'A girl has been reported missing from the Majestic Hotel in Danemouth. Her name's Ruby Keene, she's a dance <u>hostess</u> there. She didn't do her final dance last night and is still missing this morning. Go over there now. Ask for Superintendent Harper[4], and help him with anything he needs.'

In an amazingly short time Slack had arrived at Danemouth, found Superintendent Harper, interviewed the hotel manager, and was driving back to the office with Ruby Keene's cousin, Josie Turner.

'This is Josie Turner, sir,' Slack said to the Chief Constable when they arrived.

Josie was a good-looking young woman, nearer thirty than twenty. She was wearing a small amount of make-up and a dark suit. Colonel Melchett thought she looked anxious, but she was not <u>grief-stricken</u>.

As she sat down, she said: 'Do you really think it's Ruby?'

'I'm afraid that's what we need you to tell us,' replied Colonel Melchett. 'It may be rather unpleasant for you.'

After Josie had seen the body, she looked sick.

'It's Ruby,' she said. 'How horrible men are!'

'You believe it was a man?'

'Wasn't it? I just thought—'

'Any special man you were thinking of?'

She shook her head.

'No, I have no idea. Ruby wouldn't tell me if she was going out with anyone.'

Melchett said no more until they were all back at his office.

'Now, Miss Turner, I'd like to know the girl's full name and address, her relationship to you, and everything you know about her.'

'Her professional name was Ruby Keene – her real name was Rosy Legge,' replied Josie. 'Her mother was my mother's cousin. I've known her all my life but didn't see her much. She was training to be a dancer and did some theatre jobs last year. Since then she'd been working as one of the dancers at the Palais de Danse – the Dance Palace – in Brixwell, South London, but there isn't much money in it.'

'I've been dance and bridge[5] hostess at the Majestic Hotel for three years. It pays well and it's pleasant work. I have to put the right people together for bridge, and get the young people dancing with each other.'

Melchett thought that this girl would be good at her job; she seemed friendly and clever.

'As well as that,' continued Josie, 'I used to do a couple of dances every evening with Raymond Starr, the tennis and dancing professional. Well, about a month ago I fell and hurt my ankle.'

Melchett had noticed that she walked with a bit of a <u>limp</u>.

'That stopped me dancing, so I suggested to the hotel manager that Ruby could come and dance instead of me. I'd continue being the hostess but Ruby would do the dancing. I wanted to help her – and it was much better work than anything she'd done before.'

'And was she a success?'

'Oh, yes, she was quite a hit. She doesn't dance as well as I do, and she wore too much make-up – eighteen year old girls always do. That look isn't right for a place like the Majestic, so I helped her to make a few little changes.'

'And people liked her?'

'Oh, yes. Ruby wasn't very clever, though, so she was more popular with the older men than with the young ones.'

'Did she have a special friend?'

The girl's eyes met his. 'Not that *I* knew about. But then, she wouldn't tell me if she did.'

Melchett wondered why not, but he only said: 'Can you tell me when you last saw your cousin?'

'Last night. She and Raymond do two dances – one at half-past ten and the other at midnight. After the first one, I was playing bridge and I noticed Ruby dancing with one of the young men who's staying in the hotel. That's the last time I saw her. Just after midnight, Raymond came and asked me where Ruby was because she hadn't shown up for their dance. We went upstairs to her room, but she wasn't there and the dress she'd been dancing in – a big pink thing – was lying over a chair.

'We got the band to play one more song to give us time to keep looking, but there was still no Ruby, so I said to Raymond *I*'d do the dance with him. We chose one that was easy for my ankle – but it's painful this morning.

'After that we waited for her until two o'clock but she never came back. I was really angry with her.'

'And this morning you went to the police?' He knew from Slack that she had not. But he wanted to hear what she would say.

'No, I didn't. I thought Ruby had just gone out with some young man. I thought she'd come back.'

Melchett <u>pretended</u> to glance at his notes.

'Ah, yes, I see it was a Mr Jefferson who went to the police. Is he one of the guests staying at the hotel?'

'Yes.'

'What made Mr Jefferson call the police?'

Josie said rather angrily: 'Oh, he's an <u>invalid</u>. He – he gets upset rather easily.'

Melchett changed the subject. 'Who was the young man you saw your cousin dancing with?'

'George Bartlett. He's been at the hotel for about ten days.'

'Did you ask him about Ruby?'

'Yes – he said that after their dance Ruby went upstairs because she had a headache. That's when she disappeared.'

'And did Miss Keene know anybody in the village of St Mary Mead?'

'Maybe. Quite a lot of young men come into the Majestic from the village.'

'Did your cousin ever mention Gossington Hall?'

'No, I've never heard of it.' She sounded like she was being honest. There was <u>curiosity</u> in her voice too.

'Gossington Hall is where her body was found.'

'How extraordinary!'

'Do you know Colonel or Mrs Bantry?' Again Josie shook her head.

'Or Mr Basil Blake?'

She thought about it for a second.

'I think I've heard that name. But I don't remember anything about him.'

Inspector Slack passed a note to Melchett. On it was written:

'Colonel Bantry had dinner at the Majestic last week.'

Melchett didn't like Slack, but he had to admit that the Inspector worked very hard. Melchett also knew that, without saying it in words, the Inspector was warning Melchett about <u>favouring</u> his own class[1].

He turned to Josie.

'Miss Turner, please would you accompany me to Gossington Hall?'

CHAPTER 4

At Gossington Hall, Mrs Bantry and Miss Marple were chatting.

'You know,' said Mrs Bantry, 'I'm glad they've taken the body away. It's not *nice* to have a body in your house. I know you had one next door to you once, but that's not the same thing. What are you doing, Jane?'

Miss Marple was looking at her watch.

'I think I'll go home. If there's nothing more I can do for you here?'

'Oh, don't go yet,' said Mrs Bantry. 'You might miss something.'

The telephone rang and Mrs Bantry went to answer it. She was smiling when she returned.

'I told you something would happen. That was Colonel Melchett. He's bringing the poor girl's cousin here. I wonder why.'

'I think he might want her to meet Colonel Bantry,' said Miss Marple.

'To see if she recognizes him? Oh, yes, I suppose they <u>suspect</u> Arthur. But Arthur could never have had anything to do with it!'

Miss Marple smiled.

'You mustn't worry, Dolly.'

'I do a little. So does Arthur. It's made him upset. All these policemen searching the house. He's gone to the farm. Looking at pigs <u>calms</u> him when he's upset.'

A few minutes later, they saw the Chief Constable's car arrive. Colonel Melchett came in accompanied by a young woman.

'Mrs Bantry, this is Miss Turner,' he said. 'The cousin of the – the <u>victim</u>.'

'Pleased to meet you,' said Mrs Bantry. 'All this must be awful for you.'

Josie said honestly: 'Oh, none of it seems *real*, somehow.'

Mrs Bantry introduced Miss Marple, then said to Josie: 'Would you like to see where… it happened?'

Josie said after a moment: 'Yes, I think I'd like to.'

Mrs Bantry led her to the library, with Miss Marple and Melchett following.

'She was there,' said Mrs Bantry, pointing dramatically, 'on the rug.'

'Oh!' Josie <u>shivered</u>. But she also looked confused. 'I just *can't* understand it! I *can't*! It isn't the sort of place—' She stopped.

Miss Marple <u>nodded</u> her head.

'Yes,' she said quietly. 'That's what makes it so very interesting.'

Colonel Bantry was just coming in. Melchett watched Josie as he introduced them, but there was no sign on her face that she recognized him. Slack was wrong – Melchett felt very <u>relieved</u>!

Mrs Bantry wanted to know everything, so Josie told the story again of how Ruby Keene had disappeared.

'How awful for you,' said Mrs Bantry.

'I was more angry than worried,' said Josie. 'I didn't know then that anything had happened to her.'

'And yet,' said Miss Marple, 'you went to the police?'

'No, *I* didn't. That was Mr Jefferson—'

Mrs Bantry said: 'Jefferson?'

'Yes.'

'Not *Conway* Jefferson? But he's an old friend of ours. I haven't seen him for a long time. How is he?'

'Wonderful. He's always cheerful.'

'Are the family at the Majestic Hotel with him?'

'Mr Gaskell and young Mrs Jefferson and Peter? Oh, yes.'

There was something strange in Josie's voice.

Mrs Bantry said: 'They're both very nice, the young ones.'

Josie said, rather <u>uncertainly</u>:

'Oh yes – yes, they are. Yes, they are, *really*.'

'And what did she mean by that?' demanded Mrs Bantry, looking at the Chief Constable's car as it drove away, '"They are, *really*." Don't you think, Jane, that there's something—'

'Oh, I do, Dolly. I feel there is *something* about the Jeffersons that is worrying that young woman. She became different when she was talking about them. And when she talked about her cousin being missing, she said that she was *angry*! I think that's her main <u>reaction</u> to the girl's death. But *why*?'

'We'll find out!' said Mrs Bantry. 'Let's go and stay at the Majestic and you can meet Conway Jefferson. It's the saddest story. He had a son, Frank, and a daughter, Rosamund, who were both married but they still spent a lot of time with their parents. Conway's wife, too, was the sweetest woman and he loved her very much. But Conway, his wife, Frank and Rosamund were flying home from France and there was an accident. They were all killed except Conway, who lost his legs.

'But he never complains. His daughter<u>-in-law</u>, Adelaide Jefferson, lives with him – she was a <u>widow</u> when Frank Jefferson married her and she has a son, Peter Carmody, by her first marriage. And Mark Gaskell, Rosamund's husband, is there most of the time too. The whole thing was the most awful <u>tragedy</u>.'

'And now,' said Miss Marple, 'there's another tragedy...'

'Oh yes, but it's <u>nothing to do with</u> the Jeffersons.'

'Isn't it? It was Mr Jefferson who called the police.'

'So he did... You're right, Jane, that *is* strange...'

CHAPTER 5

Colonel Melchett was with Mr Prestcott, the manager of the Majestic Hotel. Also with them were Superintendent Harper of the Glenshire Police and Inspector Slack.

'So what do you know about the girl?' asked Melchett.

'Nothing,' replied Mr Prestcott. 'Josie brought her here.'

'How long has Josie worked here?'

'Two years – no, three. Josie's a good girl. She gets on with people, and when people get upset – bridge is the sort of card game where players can get upset – Josie can calm them down.'

Melchett nodded his head. He knew now what Josie reminded him of. In spite of the make-up, she seemed a lot like a teacher of young children.

'When she suggested that Ruby come to the hotel, I thought it was a good idea,' continued Mr Prestcott. 'Ruby was a bit young and not very stylish, but she danced well. People liked her.'

'Was she pretty?'

'Not really.'

'Were there many young men interested in her?'

'One or two, but no one who would strangle her, I don't think. She got on well with the older people, too – she seemed very young, I think. Still a child, really, and they liked that.'

Superintendent Harper said: 'Mr Jefferson, for instance?'

'Yes, she sat with him and his family a lot. He'd take her out for drives sometimes. I don't want any <u>misunderstanding</u>. He just likes young people around him. He's a very popular man.'

'Did his family also like her?' Melchett asked.

'They were always very pleasant to her.'

Harper said: 'And it was Mr Jefferson who reported her missing?'

The manager understood what he meant.

'*I* had no idea anything was wrong. Mr Jefferson came to my office, very upset. The girl hadn't slept in her room, he said. She must have gone for a drive and had an accident. He insisted that the police must be called at once! So yes, he called them then.'

'Did Miss Turner agree?'

'Josie was very annoyed about the whole thing – annoyed with Ruby, I mean. But what could she say?'

'I think,' said Melchett, 'we should go and see Mr Jefferson.'

Mr Prestcott went upstairs with them to Conway Jefferson's rooms. They were on the first floor, where the sea views were best. Melchett said:

'Is he a rich man?'

'Oh yes. He has the best rooms, best wines – the best of everything.'

Mr Prestcott knocked on the door and a woman's voice said: 'Come in.'

She was sitting by the window. Mr Prestcott spoke to her.

'I'm so sorry to disturb you, Mrs Jefferson, but these men would like to have a chat with Mr Jefferson. Colonel Melchett, Superintendent Harper and Inspector Slack – Mrs Jefferson.'

At first, Melchett thought that Adelaide Jefferson was a <u>plain</u> woman. Then, as she spoke, he changed his opinion. She had a charming voice and her clear, light brown eyes were beautiful. She was about thirty-five.

'My father-in-law is sleeping. This has been a terrible shock to him. The doctor gave him some pills to help him sleep. As soon as he wakes up, I know he'll want to see you. Until then, can I help?'

The policemen sat down and Mr Prestcott left the room. 'This has shocked us all very much,' Adelaide Jefferson said. 'My father-in-law was very fond of Ruby.'

Colonel Melchett asked: 'It was Mr Jefferson who reported her missing to the police?'

There was something in Adelaide Jefferson's face – what was it? Was she annoyed? Worried?

'Yes. He insisted on calling the police,' she replied.

'How well did you know Ruby Keene?' asked Melchett.

'It's difficult to say. My father-in-law is very fond of young people and liked to hear her chat. She often sat with us, and my father-in-law took her out in his car – Edwards drove, of course.'

Melchett thought: 'There are things she isn't saying.'

'Will you tell me what happened last night?' he asked.

'Certainly,' replied Adelaide. 'After dinner Ruby came and sat with us. We had arranged to play bridge, but we were waiting for Mark Gaskell, my brother-in-law, who had some important letters to write, and also for Josie.'

'Do you like Josie?'

'Yes. She's always happy and pleasant and cheerful. Although she isn't <u>well educated</u>, she has a clever mind, and she's very honest.

'So Ruby sat and talked with us for a little longer than usual. Then Josie came along, and Ruby went off to do her first dance with Raymond, the dance and tennis professional. She came back to us just as Mark joined us. Then she went to dance with a young man and Mark, Josie, my father-in-law and I started our bridge game. Then, at midnight, Raymond came to Josie, very upset, and asked where Ruby was. Josie, of course, tried to stop him talking but—'

Superintendent Harper interrupted: 'Why "of course," Mrs Jefferson?'

'Well, Josie didn't want people to know Ruby wasn't there. She felt responsible for her. She said Ruby was probably up in her bedroom, that she had said she had a headache earlier. Raymond went and called the phone in Ruby's room, but there was no answer, and he came back even more upset. So Josie danced with him. It was very brave of her, because you could see that dancing hurt her ankle. Then she came back and tried to calm Mr Jefferson, who was very upset by then. We persuaded him to go to bed. We told him Ruby had probably gone for a drive in someone's car and that they'd broken down. He went to bed and this morning he began to worry again. You know the rest.'

'Thank you. Now, do you have any idea who could have done this thing.'

'No idea at all.'

Superintendent Harper suggested that they should interview young George Bartlett and return to see Mr Jefferson later.

Colonel Melchett agreed, and the three men went out.

'Nice woman,' said the Colonel.

'Yes, very nice,' said Superintendent Harper.

George Bartlett was a young, thin man. He seemed easily confused – not someone who it was easy to get clear answers from.

'It's awful, isn't it? You read about things like this in the newspapers.'

Colonel Melchett spoke:

'How well did you know the dead girl?'

George Bartlett suddenly looked worried.

'Oh, n-n-not well at all, s-s-sir. I d-d-danced with her once or twice, chatted a bit – *you* know.'

'I think you were the last person to see her alive last night.'

'She was perfectly well when I saw her – honestly.'

'What time was that, Mr Bartlett?'

'Well, I never know about time – oh, I know, it was just after her first dance with Raymond. It must have been ten o'clock, or half past maybe?'

'Please tell us exactly what happened.'

'Well, we danced. *I'm* not much of a dancer, of course, but I talked. Ruby didn't say very much and she seemed quite tired, then she said she had a headache and went upstairs.'

'She didn't say anything about meeting someone? Or going for a drive?'

Bartlett shook his head.

'No.' He looked rather sad. 'She just left me there.'

'And what did you do when Ruby Keene left you?'

George Bartlett looked at Melchett with his mouth open.

'It's really difficult, remembering things. I think I went outside. Yes, that's it. I walked around a bit, then I came in and had a drink. I noticed Josie was dancing with the tennis man.'

'That was at midnight. You spent over an hour walking about outside?'

'Well, I was – well, I was thinking about things.'

Colonel Melchett found this hard to believe. He said:

'Have you got a car, Mr Bartlett?'

'Oh, yes.'

'Where was it? In the hotel garage?'

'No, it's outside the hotel.'

'Did you take Miss Keene for a drive?'

'Oh, no, I didn't – I promise I didn't. I didn't go for a drive at all.'

'Thank you, Mr Bartlett, I don't think we have any more questions at the moment. *At the moment*,' repeated Colonel Melchett.

They left Mr Bartlett looking scared.

'Stupid!' said Colonel Melchett. 'Or is he?'

CHAPTER 6

The night receptionist and the barman weren't very helpful. The night receptionist remembered phoning Miss Keene's room just after midnight and getting no reply. He hadn't noticed Mr Bartlett leaving or entering the hotel. Miss Keene had not gone out by the main door, but there were other stairs next to her room and a door at the end of the corridor below. She could have left the hotel without anyone seeing her.

The barman remembered Mr Bartlett being in the bar but could not remember when.

As they left the bar, they were stopped by a small boy of about nine years old.

'Excuse me, I'm Peter Carmody. Are you from the police? Do you mind me speaking to you?'

'No, that's all right, boy,' Superintendent Harper said, smiling. 'All this interests you, does it?'

'Oh yes! Will the murder be in the newspapers? You see, I'm going back to school next week and I'm going to tell everyone that I knew her *really well*.'

'What did you think of her?'

'Well, I didn't like her much. She was rather stupid. Mum and Uncle Mark didn't like her much either. She was always joining us. And they didn't like Grandfather being so nice to her. I think that they're glad she's dead,' said Peter in a cheerful voice.

'Oh, Grandfather wants to see you,' continued Peter. 'Edwards is looking for you.'

A man, dressed in a blue uniform, was walking towards them.

'Excuse me,' he said. 'I'm Edwards, Mr Jefferson's driver. He would like to see you.'

In Conway Jefferson's room, Adelaide Jefferson was talking to a tall man.

'Oh, I'm so glad you've come,' the tall man said. 'My father-in-law's been asking for you.'

This was obviously Mark Gaskell.

'Keep him as calm as you can,' said Gaskell. 'This shock could have killed him.'

Superintendent Harper said: 'I didn't know his health was bad.'

'Yes, it's his heart,' said Gaskell. 'He doesn't know, but the doctor warned Addie that if he gets over-excited or <u>startled</u>, he could die.'

Melchett said: 'Well, murder isn't exactly calming – but we'll be as careful as we can.'

Colonel Melchett had just met Mark Gaskell but already he didn't like him.

'He's handsome, but he isn't the sort of man I'd trust,' Melchett thought to himself.

Conway Jefferson was sitting in a wheelchair by the window in his big bedroom, looking at the view of the sea.

From the other side of the room, Colonel Melchett could feel how powerful the man was. He was not a weak invalid – he was a strong character. He had lots of red hair, which was turning slightly grey. His face was brown from the sun, and his eyes were a deep blue. He was clearly a man who would never complain about what he had lost; instead he would continue fighting with all his energy.

Melchett said: 'I understand, Mr Jefferson, that you knew the dead girl quite well?'

Conway Jefferson's old face smiled briefly. 'How much has my family said to you?'

'Mrs Jefferson only told us that you enjoyed chatting to the girl, and that you liked her. We haven't really spoken with Mr Gaskell yet.'

Conway Jefferson smiled again.

'Colonel Melchett, I think I should tell you some facts. Eight years ago I lost my wife, my son, my daughter and my legs. Since then I've been like a man who's lost half of himself – and I'm not speaking only about my body. I was a family man. My daughter-in-law and my son-in-law have done everything they can to be there for me. But I know that they have their own lives.

'So I'm a lonely man. I like young people, and I've been thinking about <u>adopting</u> a girl or boy. During this last month I got very friendly with the child who's been killed. She was absolutely honest. She chatted to me for hours about her life in the theatre and with her Mum and Dad as a child living in cheap accommodation. She never complained. I know she wasn't a lady, but she wasn't crude either.

'So I decided to adopt Ruby. I hope that explains my worry about her and why I called the police.'

'What did your son-in-law and daughter-in-law say when you told them your plans?' asked Superintendent Harper.

'Oh, they were fine. They don't need my money so it shouldn't matter to them. When my son Frank married, I gave half my money to him. In the same way, when my daughter Rosamund insisted on marrying a poor man, I gave her a lot of money too. That money all went to Mark when she died.'

Conway Jefferson's eyes smiled. 'They might think I'm an old fool for wanting to adopt Ruby! But I wasn't a fool. All Ruby needed was some education and she could have done anything.'

Melchett said:

'So, you were going to give the girl money – but you hadn't done this yet?'

'I understand what you're saying,' Jefferson said. 'Could someone <u>benefit</u> from the girl's death? But no, nobody could. My lawyer hadn't prepared the documents yet.'

'Then, if anything happened to you—?'

Melchett didn't finish his sentence.

'Oh, nothing's going to happen to me – I'm healthy! Still, of course I understand that accidents happen – after all, it's happened to me once before! So I made a new will[6] about ten days ago in which I left fifty thousand pounds to Ruby Keene. She would have got it when she was twenty-five.'

Harper said: 'That's a very large amount of money, Mr Jefferson. And you were leaving it to a girl you had only known for a few weeks?'

Jefferson's blue eyes suddenly looked angry.

'Well, why not? It's *my* money. *I* made it.'

'Who else gets money in your will?' Colonel Melchett asked.

'Edwards, my driver, gets a small amount and everything else goes to Mark and Addie. They would probably have got between five and ten thousand pounds each.'

'I see,' said Melchett.

'I gave most of what I had to my children. I had very little left for myself. Then, after the accident I started doing business again – and somehow, <u>everything I touched turned to gold</u>. So you see, the money I wanted to leave Ruby was completely mine – I earned it all *after* my family had died. So it was my decision what to do with it.

'And now tell me more about this terrible thing that has happened. All I know is that little Ruby was found strangled in a house twenty miles from here.'

'That's correct. Gossington Hall. Colonel Bantry's house.'

'Bantry! *Arthur* Bantry? But I know him and his wife! I met them many years ago. I didn't realize they lived near here. But why—'

He stopped and Superintendent Harper said quickly:

'Colonel Bantry had dinner here in the hotel on Tuesday last week. Did you see him?'

'Tuesday? No, we went to Harden Head that day, and had dinner on the way back.'

'Ruby Keene never mentioned the Bantrys to you?'

'Never. She didn't know anybody here, really. What's Bantry said about it?'

'He was out at a meeting last night. The body was discovered this morning and he says he's never seen the girl before.'

Superintendent Harper coughed politely. 'There's no friend from her past – no man hanging about or scaring Ruby?'

'No, she's never had a regular "boyfriend". She told me so herself.'

'Yes, I'm sure that's what she *told* you!' Superintendent Harper thought.

Jefferson continued: 'I've thought about all the men I've seen with Ruby. She had no special friend of any kind.'

Superintendent Harper tried not to show what he was thinking. The Chief Constable gave him a glance and then stood up.

'Thank you, Mr Jefferson. That's all we need for now.'

The two men left and Conway Jefferson called: 'Edwards!'

The driver appeared.

'Yes, sir?'

'Call <u>Sir</u> Henry Clithering. Ask him to come here today if he can. Tell him it's urgent.'

CHAPTER 7

When they were outside Jefferson's door, Superintendent Harper said:

'Well, we've got a <u>motive</u>, sir.'

'Hmm,' said Melchett. 'Fifty thousand pounds? But—'

Colonel Melchett didn't finish his sentence. But Harper understood what he meant.

'You don't think it's likely in this situation? No, neither do I. But we've got to look at it anyway. We need to look at Mr Gaskell's and Mrs Jefferson's <u>finances</u> – but there's another possibility that I think is much more likely.'

Melchett said: 'A boyfriend of Ruby's?'

'That's it, sir. Someone she knew before she came here. This plan to adopt Ruby – maybe her boyfriend found out about it, he thought he would lose her and he went mad with anger.'

'But why was she in Bantry's library?'

'Well, perhaps the boyfriend killed her in his car, and he didn't know how to get rid of the body. Maybe they were near the gates of a big house at the time. He thinks, "if she was found there the attention would be on the house and the people who live there". So he breaks a window, climbs in and puts her down on the rug. There's no blood in the car because he strangled her – so there's no <u>evidence</u>. Do you see what I mean, sir?'

'Oh – er – c-could I speak to you?' It was George Bartlett.

Colonel Melchett, who wanted to see what progress Inspector Slack had made in Ruby's bedroom, was a little rude:

'Well, what is it?'

'Well, I – I can't find my car.'

Colonel Melchett tried to be patient.

'What type is it?'

'It's a Minoan.'

'And when did you last see it?'

'Before lunch yesterday. I was going to go for a drive in the afternoon. But somehow I went to sleep instead.'

'And the car was outside the hotel?'

'I suppose so. I mean, that's where I'd put it.'

'Would you have noticed if it had *not* been there?'

Mr Bartlett shook his head.

'I don't think so. There were lots of cars coming and going. Plenty of Minoans.'

Superintendent Harper nodded his head. Looking out of the window, he saw that at that moment, there were eight Minoans outside the hotel.

Superintendent Harper said to Colonel Melchett: 'I'll join you upstairs in a moment, sir. I'll just get someone to take a <u>statement</u> from Mr Bartlett.'

Josie Turner and Ruby Keene had had rooms at the end of a dark little corridor. Melchett saw at once what the night receptionist had meant – it would be easy to leave the hotel from Ruby Keene's room without anyone seeing, using the side stairs and door.

◆ ◆ ◆

Inspector Slack had been busy looking for <u>clues</u> in Ruby's room.

The Glenshire police had already looked for <u>fingerprints</u>, but there were only Ruby's, Josie's, and the cleaner's. There were also a couple of fingerprints made by Raymond Starr, but he had said that he had come up with Josie to look for Ruby.

Slack found nothing interesting – just bills, receipts, old cinema and theatre tickets, a few newspaper articles and beauty advice pages from magazines, and some letters from someone called Lil, a friend from the Palais de Danse. Lil mentioned the names of various men who were missing Ruby.

Slack had written down all the names Lil mentioned.

On a chair in the middle of the room was the pink dance dress Ruby had worn early in the evening. There were matching pink shoes on the floor. The wardrobe door was open and showed a variety of rather cheap evening dresses. There were some dirty clothes in a basket in the corner. In the bin, he found some fingernail <u>clippings</u>, and old face-cleaning tissues with red make-up and <u>nail polish</u> on them. The facts seemed clear: Ruby Keene had gone upstairs, changed her clothes and hurried out again – but *where*?

Josie Turner knew most about Ruby's life and friends, and she couldn't help. But Inspector Slack could understand why this might be:

'If it's true about this plan to adopt Ruby, she would keep quiet about seeing an old boyfriend, because Josie would stop her. So the boyfriend comes down here, Ruby goes out without telling anyone, he gets angry and strangles her.'

'You're probably right, Slack,' said Colonel Melchett, 'Well, we should be able to discover who this male friend is fairly easily.'

'You leave it to me, sir,' said Slack. 'I'll contact this Lil. We'll soon get the truth.'

◆ ◆ ◆

Superintendent Harper knew what Raymond Starr looked like. He was tall, slim, and good-looking, with very white teeth. He was very popular in the hotel.

'I can't help you much, Superintendent. Ruby was pleasant – and rather stupid. A few young men in the hotel were interested in her, but nothing special. She was nearly always with the Jefferson family.'

'Did you know that Mr Jefferson was going to adopt Ruby?' Harper asked.

'The clever little girl!' Starr smiled. 'Oh, well, there's <u>no fool like an old fool</u>.'

'Ruby never mentioned that to you?'

'No. I knew she was happy about something, but I didn't know what it was.'

'And Josie?'

'Oh, she was probably the one who planned the whole thing. She's clever, that girl.'

Harper nodded his head. It was Josie who had asked Ruby to come to the hotel; Josie had probably encouraged the friendship. Then Ruby had not appeared for her dance and Conway Jefferson had begun to worry. Josie could see all her plans about to go wrong. It wasn't surprising that she had been upset.

'Did Ruby ever mention someone she had known in London coming to see her here? Or someone she had had problems with – you know the sort of thing I mean?'

'I understand perfectly,' said Starr, 'but <u>as far as I know</u>, there was no one. She certainly never said anything.'

'Thank you, Mr Starr. Now, please can you tell me what happened last night?'

'Certainly. Ruby and I did our dance at ten-thirty and I didn't notice what happened afterwards because I had my own dancing partners to look after. At midnight Ruby hadn't come back so I went to Josie, who was playing bridge with the Jeffersons. She didn't know where Ruby was, and I saw she was worried that Mr Jefferson would get upset. I asked the band to play another dance. Then I went to the office and asked them to call Ruby's room. She didn't answer so I went back to Josie. She suggested that Ruby was perhaps asleep, so we went upstairs together to look for her.'

'And what did she say when she was alone with you?'

'She looked very angry and said: "Stupid little fool. She can't do this sort of thing. It will <u>ruin</u> all her chances. Who's she with, do you know?" I said that I didn't know. The last time I'd seen her she was dancing with Bartlett. Josie said: "She wouldn't be with *him*. What *can* she be doing? She isn't with that film man, is she?"'

Harper said quickly: '*Film man?* Who was he?'

Raymond said: 'I don't know his name. He's got black hair and looks a bit different. He works in the film industry – or that's what he told Ruby. He had dinner here once or twice and danced with Ruby, but I don't think she knew him well. I told Josie that I didn't think he'd been here tonight and she said: "Well, she must be out with *someone*. What am I going to say to the Jeffersons?"'

'We got to Ruby's room and the dress she had been wearing was lying across a chair but Ruby wasn't there. Josie said *she'd* dance with me instead. So she went and changed her dress and we went downstairs and did a dance. After that she asked me to help her calm the Jeffersons – she said it was important. So I did.'

Superintendent Harper nodded his head. 'Thank you, Mr Starr.'

He watched as Raymond Starr walked away down the steps of the <u>terrace</u>, picking up a bag of tennis balls and a racket on the way. Mrs Jefferson, also carrying a racket, joined him and they went towards the tennis courts.

At that moment, a police officer arrived at Harper's side.

'Excuse me, sir. A message has just arrived. A <u>burnt-out</u> car has been found about two miles from here. They think there is a burnt body inside.'

'Could they read the <u>registration number</u> of the car?'

'No, sir. But they think they will be able to find the owner using the engine number. They think it's a Minoan.'

CHAPTER 8

'Good, I'm glad you've come,' Conway Jefferson said.

'What's the matter?' Sir Henry Clithering asked.

'Murder's the matter. I'm involved in it and so are the Bantrys.'

'Arthur and Dolly Bantry?' Clithering sounded surprised.

Jefferson told him the facts.

'It's all very strange,' Sir Henry said when Jefferson had finished. Then Sir Henry, who had been Commissioner of the London Police[4], asked: 'How are the Bantrys involved, do you think?'

'I think the fact that I know them is the only <u>connection</u>,' replied Jefferson. 'The Bantrys said they had never seen the girl before, so isn't it possible that someone killed her and then <u>deliberately</u> left her body in my friends' house?'

'I think that's unlikely. But what do you want *me* to do?'

Jefferson said: 'I'm an invalid. I can't <u>investigate</u>. Do you know Melchett, the Chief Constable of Radfordshire?'

'Yes, I've met him.'

When he heard the name, Sir Henry was reminded of something. He remembered a face he'd just seen downstairs in the hotel, a face that he was sure was connected to the last time he had seen Melchett…

'Conway, I don't investigate any more.'

'I know and not being in the police any more makes things simpler,' Jefferson said.

'That's true – if I were still working I wouldn't be able to help at all. This isn't my part of the country.'

'But your experience,' said Jefferson, 'means you are interested in the <u>case</u>, and the police may be grateful for your help.'

Sir Henry said slowly: 'I don't know if you need me. You've got an expert at solving mysteries sitting downstairs. She's better at it than I am. She's an old lady with a sweet face – and a mind that knows all about the bad in people. Her name's Miss Marple. She comes from the village of St Mary Mead and she's a friend of the Bantrys' – if you have a crime that needs solving, then she's the person you need, Conway.'

'You're joking.'

'No, I'm not. The last time I saw Melchett, a girl had killed herself. Then old Miss Marple gets involved. She says she hasn't got any evidence, but she knows it was murder – the girl didn't kill herself – and she knows who the murderer is. She gives me a piece of paper with a name on it. And she was right!'

'How?' Jefferson said. He didn't sound like he believed Sir Henry.

'Specialized knowledge. We use it in police work too. For example, when we want to catch a burglar, we can usually guess which one it was because we know how each of the local burglars acts. In the same way, Miss Marple makes interesting connections between people and events in a crime and life in her village.'

'But what is she likely to know about a girl who's probably never been to a village in her life?'

'Oh, I think,' said Sir Henry, 'that she might have some interesting ideas.'

Miss Marple looked happy when she saw Sir Henry approaching.

'Oh, Sir Henry, this is lucky – meeting you here.'

Sir Henry was charming. 'It's a great pleasure, Miss Marple. Are you staying here?'

'We are. Mrs Bantry's here too.' She looked at him. 'I can see you've heard the news about the body. It's terrible, isn't it?'

'Yes,' agreed Sir Henry. 'But I imagine that Dolly's almost enjoying herself and she's brought you along to solve the mystery for her? Have you got any ideas?'

'Oh, I don't know very much about it yet.'

'I can change that. I'm going to ask you to help me, Miss Marple.'

He briefly told her the facts and Miss Marple listened with interest.

'Poor Mr Jefferson,' Miss Marple said. 'To leave him alive, disabled and without his family, seems more cruel than if he had been killed too.'

'Yes. The thing I can't understand, though, is the sudden feeling for this girl.'

'I think he was just looking for a nice girl to take his dead daughter's place, and this girl saw her opportunity! I've seen so many cases like this.

'There was Mr Badger who had the chemist's shop. He was particularly kind to the young lady who worked in his shop. He told his wife that they must think of her as a daughter and let her come and live in their house.'

Sir Henry said: 'If Ruby Keene had only been a girl from his own class[1]—'

Miss Marple interrupted him.

'Oh! But that wouldn't have been nearly as good from his point of view. It's like the story of King Cophetua[7].

'If you're a lonely, tired old man, and if your own family have stopped noticing you, well, to make friends with someone who will be <u>overwhelmed</u> by you, that makes you feel a much greater person – a generous king! Mr Badger bought the girl in his shop an expensive bracelet. However, Mrs Badger decided to investigate. And when she told Mr Badger that the girl had a young boyfriend, and had sold the bracelet to give him the money – well, the relationship ended. He gave Mrs Badger an expensive ring the following Christmas...'

Her clever eyes met Sir Henry's.

'Are you suggesting that if there had been a young man in Ruby's life, Conway's attitude towards her might have changed?'

'Well, I definitely think that if Ruby had had a young man she wouldn't have told him.'

'And the young man might not have liked that?'

'That *is* the most obvious solution. I did also think that her cousin, Josie Turner, who was at Gossington this morning, looked *angry* with the dead girl. But what you've told me explains *why*. She was probably hoping to become very rich through Ruby's arrangement.'

'Is she rather <u>cold</u>?'

'I don't know. The poor thing has had to work for her money, so of course she doesn't care much that if Jefferson adopted Ruby, it would mean that a rich man and woman – Mr Gaskell and Mrs Jefferson – were going to lose some money. In her eyes, they never earned it. I think Miss Turner is an <u>ambitious</u> young woman who enjoys life. A little like Jessie Golden, the baker's daughter,' added Miss Marple.

'What happened to her?' asked Sir Henry.

'She trained as a teacher, got a job working for a rich family in a big house, and then married the son.'

Sir Henry nodded his head.

'Is there any reason why you think my friend Conway should suddenly have become like this "King Cophetua"?'

'Well, he had a terrible shock and lost his family. But, as my dear mother used to say, time is a great <u>healer</u>. Mr Gaskell and

Mrs Jefferson are young. They probably want to move forward. They might even want to get married again. And Mr Jefferson may have started to feel unnecessary. Men so *easily* feel that way.'

'Well,' said Sir Henry, 'I don't like the way you think all men are the same.'

Miss Marple shook her head in a sad way.

'Human nature is the same everywhere, Sir Henry.'

Miss Marple looked very serious as she said: 'Sir Henry, there's a great possibility that this crime will be one of those that never gets solved. But if that happens, it will be absolutely awful for the Bantrys. Colonel Bantry won't notice it for a while, but people will refuse his invitations and make excuses, and slowly he will understand.'

'You mean that people will think that *he* was involved?'

'Of course! And people will avoid the Bantrys. That's why we have to find out what really happened, and why I came here with Mrs Bantry. People talking about them will be so painful for them. So you see, we've *got* to find out the truth.'

'Do you have any idea why the body was found in the Bantrys' house?' asked Sir Henry. 'There must be an explanation – a connection. Do you think someone took her out in a car, strangled her and then quickly decided to push her into the first house he saw?'

'No. I think there was a very careful plan. What happened was that the plan went wrong.'

Sir Henry was interested.

'Why did the plan go wrong?'

Miss Marple said:

'Strange things happen, don't they? This particular plan went wrong because human beings are so much more <u>sensitive</u> than we think. It doesn't sound sensible, but that's what I believe and—'

She stopped. 'Here's Mrs Bantry now.'

CHAPTER 9

Mrs Bantry was with Adelaide Jefferson. She came up to Sir Henry and said in a surprised voice: '*You?*'

He took both her hands. 'I can't tell you how upset I am about all this.'

Mrs Bantry, however, didn't seem even slightly upset. 'Miss Marple and I have come here to be detectives,' she said happily. 'Do you know Mrs Jefferson?'

'Yes, of course.' He smiled at Adelaide politely.

Mrs Bantry said:

'Let's go out onto the terrace and have drinks and talk about it all.'

The four of them went out and joined Mark Gaskell.

'We *can* talk about it, can't we?' said Mrs Bantry. 'We're all old friends – except Miss Marple. She's a new friend but she knows all about crime, and she wants to help. Now, Addie, what was she really like, this girl? Did you like her?'

'No, of course I didn't.' Adelaide looked a little embarrassed, so Mrs Bantry decided to ask Mark Gaskell instead.

'What was she really like?'

'A gold-digger,' he said at once.

'But couldn't you *do* something about it?' asked Mrs Bantry.

'We might have, if we'd realized it in time,' Mark said.

He looked at Adelaide and her cheeks turned red.

'Mark thinks I should have seen what was happening.'

'You left him alone too much, Addie. You were too busy having tennis lessons and everything else. And Jeff has always been such a sensible old man.' They both called their father-in-law 'Jeff'.

'Men are frequently not as sensible as they seem,' said Miss Marple, talking about the opposite sex like a wild animal.

'Very true,' said Mark. 'Unfortunately, we thought there was no <u>harm</u> in her. No harm in her! Now I wish I'd hurt her myself!'

'Mark,' said Addie, 'you really *must* be careful what you say.'

He smiled.

'Or people will think I actually *did* hurt her? Oh, I suppose the police already suspect me. If anyone wanted that girl dead it was Addie and me.'

'Mark!' cried Adelaide.

'All right, all right,' said Mark. 'She's dead, poor little thing. And why shouldn't she try to make Jeff like her? Who am I to judge? I've done plenty of bad things myself.'

Sir Henry said: 'What did you say when Conway told you he was going to adopt the girl?'

'What could we say? Jeff's always been good to us. We couldn't say anything.'

Adelaide said: 'If it had been some other kind of girl... well, we would have *understood* it. And Jeff's always seemed so fond of Peter.'

'Of course,' said Mrs Bantry. 'I'd quite forgotten Peter was your first husband's child. I've always thought of him as Mr Jefferson's grandson.'

'So have I,' said Adelaide. Her voice made Miss Marple turn and look at her.

'It was Josie's fault,' said Mark. 'Josie brought her here.'

Adelaide said:

'Oh, but you don't think she deliberately brought Ruby to meet Jeff, do you?'

'No, but she probably saw what was happening between Jeff and Ruby long before we did and kept very quiet about it.'

Mrs Bantry asked:

'Was Ruby very pretty? I saw her – her body. But it was impossible to...'

Mark said:

'She wasn't pretty without make-up. She had a thin, little face, not much chin, teeth pointing into her mouth – but with make-up she managed to look okay. Her hair was dyed, of course. Actually, I hadn't thought of it before, but with all the make-up and dyed hair she looked a little like my wife Rosamund. I'm sure that's why the old man liked her. The awful thing is that Addie and I are glad that she's dead—'

He stopped, and looked towards the doors.

'Well, well – look who's here.'

Mrs Jefferson got up and walked quickly along the terrace to a tall, middle-aged man with a thin brown face.

Mrs Bantry said: 'Isn't that Hugo McLean?'

'Yes, he's as <u>devoted</u> as a dog to Addie,' said Mark. 'Addie's only got to smile and Hugo comes running. He hopes that she'll marry him. I suppose she phoned him this morning.'

Edwards came along the terrace and approached Mark.

'Excuse me, sir. Mr Jefferson would like you to come to his rooms.'

Mark said: 'See you later,' and went inside. Sir Henry said quietly to Miss Marple: 'Well, what do you think of the people who will benefit most from the crime?'

Miss Marple thought for a moment:

'I think Mrs Jefferson is a very devoted mother. She's the kind of woman everyone likes. The kind of woman that many men would want to marry.'

Sir Henry laughed. 'And Mark Gaskell? You don't like him, do you, Miss Marple?'

'Oh yes, I do,' she replied. 'Most women would like him. But he doesn't <u>fool</u> me.'

A tall, dark-haired young man came onto the terrace and paused for a minute, watching Adelaide Jefferson and Hugo McLean.

'That's the tennis and dancing professional, Raymond Starr,' said Sir Henry.

Miss Marple said: 'He's very good-looking, isn't he? I think Mrs Jefferson said that she'd been having tennis lessons...'

Young Peter Carmody came across the terrace and spoke to Sir Henry.

'Somebody told me you were the head of the London police. Do you know who did the murder yet?'

'Not yet,' replied Sir Henry, smiling.

'Are you enjoying this, Peter?' asked Mrs Bantry.

'I am! I've been looking around to see if I can find any clues, but I haven't been lucky. I've got a souvenir, though. Mother wanted me to throw it away but I'm not going to.'

He took a small box from his pocket. Opening it, he showed the adults the contents.

'It's a fingernail. *Her* fingernail! I'm going to make a label: *Fingernail of the Murdered Woman* and take it back to school. It's a good souvenir, don't you think?'

'Where did you get it?' asked Miss Marple.

'Before dinner last night Ruby broke her nail on Josie's scarf. Mum cut it off for her and gave it to me and said put it in the wastepaper basket, but I put it in my pocket and then forgot about it. This morning I remembered, so now I've got it as a souvenir.'

'Have you got any other souvenirs?' asked Sir Henry.

Peter pulled out an envelope and took out something brown.

'It's a bit of George Bartlett's <u>shoelace</u>,' he explained. 'I saw his shoes outside his door this morning and I took a bit, just in case he's the murderer. He was the last person to see her. Look, there's Uncle Hugo. I suppose Mum asked him to come. She always does if she's in trouble. Look! There's Josie. Hi, Josie!'

Josie turned around. She looked surprised to see Mrs Bantry and Miss Marple, but she came over to say hello.

Sir Henry said: 'Do you mind me asking you a question, Miss Turner? Have Mrs Jefferson and Mr Gaskell been unpleasant to you about the Ruby thing? I don't mean the murder – but the plan to adopt her.'

Josie said: 'They haven't *said* anything. But I think they blamed me for Mr Jefferson liking Ruby so much. I think they thought I had planned it. But I never imagined someone like Mr Jefferson would want to adopt a girl like Ruby – it was a complete surprise to me.'

Her words sounded honest.

'It was lucky for Ruby, wasn't it? Everyone should be allowed to have luck sometimes.'

She looked at them, thinking, and then went on into the hotel.

'I don't think *she* did it,' Peter said.

Miss Marple said quietly: 'It's interesting, that piece of fingernail. Her nails had been worrying me, you know.'

'Her nails?' asked Sir Henry.

'Yes, the dead girl's nails,' said Mrs Bantry. 'They were quite *short*, and now that Jane says so, of course it *was* a little strange. A girl like that usually has long nails.'

Miss Marple said: 'But if she had to cut one off, then she might cut the others to match it. Did they find any nail clippings in her room?'

'I'll ask Superintendent Harper when he gets back,' said Sir Henry. 'But I'm afraid there's been another tragedy. A burnt-out car—'

Miss Marple was shocked. 'Was there someone in the car?'

'I'm afraid so, yes.'

'I expect that will be the Girl Guide who's missing, Pamela Reeves,' Miss Marple said.

Sir Henry said:

'Now why do you think that, Miss Marple?'

'Well, it was reported on the radio that she was missing. And she lived in Daneleigh Vale, which isn't very far from here. And she was last seen at a Girl Guides meeting up on Danebury Downs. She'd have to go through Danemouth to get home. Maybe she saw or heard something that no one was meant to see and hear. If so, she'd have to be... removed.'

Sir Henry said: 'You think there was a second murder?'

'Well, why not?' Her eyes met his. 'When someone has murdered one person, it isn't as hard to murder another. Or even a third person.'

'Miss Marple, you worry me,' said Sir Henry. 'Do you think there's going to be a *third* murder? And do you know *who* is going to be murdered?'

'Yes and yes, I think I do.'

◆ ◆ ◆

Superintendent Harper was looking at the burnt-out car, talking to one of his police sergeants.

'Well, sir,' said the officer. 'Petrol was poured over the car and the whole thing was <u>set alight</u>. There are three empty petrol cans over there.'

Another policeman was looking at some small objects from the burnt car. There was a black shoe and some small pieces of material. As Harper approached, the policeman looked up.

'It must be her, sir. This is a button from a Girl Guide's uniform...'

Harper felt sick. First Ruby Keene and now this child, Pamela Reeves. He would not rest until he had found the man or woman who had killed them.

CHAPTER 10

Colonel Melchett and Superintendent Harper looked at each other.

'We've got two murders,' said Melchett. 'Ruby Keene and Pamela Reeves. Do you think they're connected?'

'Oh, I think they definitely are,' Harper replied. 'Pamela Reeves went to a Girl Guides meeting on Danebury Downs. Her friends at Girl Guides say she was normal and cheerful. But she didn't go home with them. She said that she was going into Danemouth to visit Woolworth's shop. If that's true, she went past the Majestic Hotel. So, it's possible that she heard or saw Ruby Keene, and the murderer had to kill her too.'

Colonel Melchett said: 'But Pamela Reeves couldn't have been near the Majestic at eleven o'clock at night, which is when the murder happened. She must have been there earlier in the evening, so perhaps she heard somebody making plans – maybe she heard Ruby arranging to meet someone later that evening. Which means that the murder of Ruby Keene was <u>premeditated</u>.'

'I believe it was, sir. I don't think you can explain Pamela's death otherwise. And the car is the connection between her death and the Majestic Hotel. It *was* Mr George Bartlett's car. Bartlett is either a very clever man pretending to be a fool, or – well, he *is* a fool.'

'Mmmm,' agreed Melchett, thinking. 'What we need is a motive. Bartlett had no motive to kill Ruby Keene.'

'Yes, motive is a problem. Did we find out anything interesting when Slack talked to the people at the Palais de Danse?'

'No, nothing at all. Slack says that all of Ruby's most frequent dancing partners have <u>alibis</u> for that night.'

'Ah,' said Harper.

'I have news on the daughter- and son-in-law,' he continued. 'Mr Conway Jefferson may think that Mr Gaskell and Mrs Jefferson have enough money, but in fact they're both poor. Jefferson's son lost most of the money his father gave him. I think Mrs Jefferson has found it difficult to pay for her son to go to a good school.'

'Hasn't she asked her father-in-law for help?'

'No, sir. He doesn't know anything about it.'

'Now Mr Gaskell. He lost all his wife's money playing cards. He needs money badly, so they both had a motive. But they both have an alibi too. They *couldn't* have done it.

'After dinner, Mr Gaskell told everyone that he had to write some letters and left. He told me he just didn't want to play bridge for another whole evening, so he used the letters as an excuse. Actually he went for a drive in his car. When he returned, Ruby Keene was dancing with Raymond. After the dance Ruby had a drink with them, then she went to dance with Bartlett. Gaskell and the others started playing bridge.

'That was at twenty minutes to eleven, and Gaskell didn't leave the table until after midnight. Everyone says so. The family, the waiters, *everyone*. And Mrs Jefferson's alibi is the same – she was playing bridge until midnight. So they can't have killed Ruby. That is, if she *was* killed before midnight.'

'If Dr Haydock says she was, then she was,' said the Colonel. He also says she was <u>drugged</u> before she was strangled. We must think about that too.'

Harper returned to his list of <u>suspects</u>: 'Basil Blake. Well, he lives near Gossington Hall and works at Lemville Studios. He had dinner at the Majestic quite often and he danced with the girl. Do you remember what Josie said to Raymond? "She's not with that film man, is she?" She meant Blake. But he was at a work party that night. Inspector Slack says Blake left the party at about midnight. The young woman who is at his house – Miss Dinah Lee – says that is correct. And at midnight Ruby Keene was already dead.'

'Where was the party?'

'Thirty miles south-west of London.'

'Hmm, so he wasn't nearby at all.' Colonel Melchett was confused. 'This is useless!'

'George Bartlett's our best hope,' continued Harper. 'If we had a motive for him. His mother died a year ago and he got all her money. He's spending it very quickly, but he isn't poor yet. But could he murder someone for money?'

Melchett was quiet for a moment, then he said: 'So, where are we?'

'Nowhere, sir,' said Superintendent Harper.

CHAPTER 11

'I like your friend,' said Adelaide Jefferson to Mrs Bantry.

The two women were sitting on the terrace.

'Yes, Jane Marple's amazing,' Mrs Bantry said. 'People call her a <u>busybody</u>, but she isn't really.'

'She just doesn't have a good opinion of people?'

'You could call it that.'

'That's quite nice for a change,' said Adelaide, 'after Jeff having too good an opinion of Ruby for so long. She was nice, but she was a little gold-digger. She knew how to make a lonely, elderly man like her.'

'Mmm,' said Mrs Bantry, thinking. 'I suppose Conway *is* lonely.'

'Oh yes, he has been this summer. I – I've had such a strange life. Mike Carmody, my first husband, died soon after we were married and Peter, as you know, was born after his death. Mike's best friend was Frank Jefferson. So I saw a lot of him and after Mike died, we grew very close. Then finally, he asked me to marry him.'

She paused, then continued: 'It sounds strange… Frank's father and mother were so nice to him. Yet… Jeff is a very strong character, and when you live with a strong character, you can't have a character of your own. Frank felt that.

'When we got married, Jeff gave Frank a lot of money. Frank wanted to be clever with money like his father. And, of course, he wasn't. So when he died, there was very little money left for me and Peter. I – I didn't tell Jeff because it wasn't fair to Frank. So Jeff still thinks that I'm rich.

'We've been like a family all these years. But Jeff doesn't think of me as Frank's *widow* – he still thinks of me as Frank's *wife*, and to him Mark is Rosamund's husband. But suddenly, this summer, I didn't want to think of Frank any more!

'I want to be me – Addie. Hugo wants to marry me and this summer, I decided that I want to marry him too... So when Ruby appeared, I was glad. Jeff was happy. I could live my own life. But I never imagined that he would want to – to *adopt* her!'

'And how did you feel when you found out?'

'I was shocked! Angry, too. You see, Peter needs Jeff's money – so a gold-digging little fool getting it all instead? Oh, I could have killed her!'

She stopped, suddenly. *'What an awful thing to say!'*

Hugo McLean heard her as he arrived. 'What's an awful thing to say?' he asked.

'That I could have killed Ruby Keene.'

Hugo McLean was quiet for a moment. Then he said:

'No, I wouldn't say that if I were you. People might not understand what you mean.

'You've got to be more careful, Addie.' There was a warning in his voice.

Mark Gaskell was talking with Sir Henry Clithering.

'I've just realized that I'm Suspect Number One!' Mark Gaskell was not happy. 'The police have found out about my money problems. The doctors think dear old Jeff will die within a month or two. When he does, Addie and I each get half of his money, then everything will be OK for me. Otherwise... well, I owe a lot of people a lot of money – and they want it back.

'So honestly, it's lucky for me that somebody strangled Ruby before she got all his money. *I* couldn't murder anybody, of course. But I can't ask the police to believe that! I'm surprised that I'm not in jail already!'

'Well, you've got an alibi,' Sir Henry said.

Mark laughed. 'No <u>innocent</u> person ever has an alibi!'

'It's good to be able to joke about it.'

'Actually, I'm scared. Murder is scary!'

'Yes, it is,' Sir Henry agreed.

'I do feel sorry for Jeff, you know. But it's better this way than if he'd ever found out that Ruby was lying to him.

'I'm very fond of Jeff,' Mark continued, 'and at the same time I hate him. Jeff is a man who likes to be in control. He's kind, generous – but he plays the music and we dance to it.'

Mark paused.

'I loved my wife. I'll never love anyone else as much. I don't want to marry again. But I like women and I want a life. I've had fun when Jeff couldn't see me. But poor Addie hasn't. To Jeff, she's still Frank's wife and it's like being in prison. But this summer, Addie began to act like a free woman again and it shocked him. The result of that shock was Ruby Keene.'

Despite what Mark Gaskell said, Sir Henry didn't think that he seemed at all sorry about Ruby Keene's death.

It was no surprise, he thought, that the police were interested in him.

CHAPTER 12

Dr Metcalf had just finished examining Conway Jefferson.

'Mr Jefferson's health is not good, Superintendent Harper. He is an invalid, but he still refuses to rest, to relax. His heart is working too hard.'

'How much of an invalid is he?' Harper asked.

'His arms and shoulders are very strong. He can move his wheelchair independently. So he is fit, but a sudden shock could kill him.'

'But a shock *didn't* kill him. The murder was a big shock.'

Dr Metcalf nodded his head.

'In my experience, a <u>*physical*</u> shock is often more likely to kill someone than a <u>*mental*</u> shock. For example, the loud noise of a door closing suddenly would be more likely to kill Mr Jefferson than finding out about the murder of a girl he was fond of. A physical shock makes the heart jump – that could kill him.'

Superintendent Harper said slowly: 'But not everyone knows the difference? Someone might *think* that the shock of Ruby's death would kill Mr Jefferson?'

'Yes, I suppose so.'

♦ ◆ ♦

Later on, Harper was discussing the case with Sir Henry Clithering. 'You must admit, sir, that the two events would <u>kill two birds with one stone</u>. First the girl's death, and then the fact of her death kills Mr Jefferson too... Now, I know that they're friends of yours, so you will know: just how fond is Mr Jefferson of Mr Gaskell and Mrs Jefferson? Does he like them as people, or does he love them because they're family? What do you think would happen if one of them married again?'

Sir Henry thought about this for a moment.

'I think he's fond of Mrs Jefferson. But honestly, if they married again, I think that he would have no more interest in them.'

Superintendent Harper nodded his head.

'Would you mind if we walked along to the tennis court? Miss Marple's sitting there and I want you and her to do something for me. I want you to talk to Edwards, sir. Conway Jefferson's driver.'

'What do you want from Edwards?'

'I want to know everything he knows about the relationships between the various members of the family, and what he thinks about the Ruby Keene murder. He knows better than anyone what's going on with the family– and he wouldn't tell me. But he'll tell *you*. That is, of course, if you don't mind?'

Sir Henry said seriously: 'No, I don't mind. How do you want Miss Marple to help you?'

'I'd like her to help with the Girl Guides. I don't think Pamela Reeves went to Woolworth's, and I want to know where she was really going. She may have said something to her friends. If so, Miss Marple's the person to find out.'

Miss Marple listened to the Superintendent's request and at once agreed to help.

'I think you're right – I *could* be useful. I've got quite a lot of experience with girls. I know when a girl is telling the truth and when she's lying. I see so much in the village.'

'Oh, and Miss Marple,' said Sir Henry, 'the Superintendent tells me that there *were* nail clippings in Ruby's wastepaper basket.'

'Why did you want to know, Miss Marple?' asked Harper.

'Her hands were one of the things that seemed *wrong* when I looked at the body. But I couldn't think *why*. Then I realized that girls who wear a lot of make-up usually have very long fingernails. Then Peter said something that showed that her nails *had* been long, but she broke one. So then, of course, she might have cut the rest, and that's why I asked about clippings.'

'You said "*one* of the things" that seemed wrong when you looked at the body. Was there something else?' Sir Henry asked.

'Oh, the dress. It was an old dress, not very nice. Now that's all wrong.'

'I don't see why.'

Miss Marple went a little pink.

'Well, the idea is that Ruby Keene changed her dress and went to meet someone who she liked a lot. She would have wanted to look her best. So why was she wearing an old dress? She'd wear her best dress. That's what girls do.'

'Maybe she was going to meet this man outside. Maybe they were going for a walk. Then she'd put on an old dress.'

'Then the sensible thing to do would be to change into trousers and a jumper,' said Miss Marple. 'And I don't want to be rude, but it's what a girl of – of our class would do[1].'

'Ruby, however, belonged to the class that wear their best clothes to meet someone special. She'd have kept on the dress she was wearing – her best pink one.'

'So what's your explanation for all this, Miss Marple?' Harper asked.

'I haven't got one yet. But I feel that these are important clues…'

Raymond Starr had just finished teaching a tennis lesson when Sir Henry and Miss Marple arrived at the tennis court. He smiled at his pupil, and then shook his head as she left:

'She'll never be able to play.'

'All this must be very boring for you,' said Miss Marple.

'It is, sometimes.'

There was something Sir Henry didn't like about Raymond Starr.

'You come from Devonshire[1], don't you, sir?' said Raymond to Sir Henry. 'I come from Alsmonston.'

Sir Henry looked surprised.

'Are you one of the Devonshire Starrs[1]? I didn't realize that.'

Then Sir Henry felt embarrassed.

'It was bad luck, all that,' he said.

'You mean having to sell the house that my family had lived in for three hundred years? Yes, it was, and it's hard to get a job nowadays when the only thing you've got is a public-school education[8]! The only things I could do were dance and play tennis. So that's exactly what I do.' He laughed.

Sir Henry smiled at him, then said:

'We wanted to talk to you.'

'About Ruby Keene? She didn't tell me anything.'

Miss Marple said: 'Did you like her?'

'Not particularly. I didn't dislike her.' He didn't seem interested in the conversation. 'It just seems to be a horrible little mystery – no clues, no motive.'

'Two people had a motive,' said Miss Marple.

'Really?' Raymond looked surprised.

Sir Henry said, 'Mrs Jefferson and Mr Gaskell will probably get fifty thousand pounds now that Ruby is dead.'

'What?' Raymond looked shocked and upset. 'Oh, but that's impossible! Mrs Jefferson? Or Mr Gaskell? No, they couldn't have strangled a girl...' He shook his head.

Miss Marple said gently:

'I'm afraid you're too nice, Mr Starr. Money is a very powerful motive.'

Raymond stood up.

'Here's Mrs Jefferson now. She's come for her tennis lesson!'

Adelaide Jefferson and Hugo McLean were walking down the path towards them.

Smiling, Addie went onto the tennis court. McLean watched her laughing with Raymond.

'I don't know why Addie wants to have tennis lessons,' he said. 'And who *is* this Raymond?'

'He's one of the Devonshire Starrs,' said Sir Henry.

'What?'

Sir Henry nodded his head. Hugo McLean looked even more unhappy.

'I don't know why Addie asked me to come here,' he said. 'She doesn't seem at all upset.'

Sir Henry asked: 'When did she ask you to come?'

'Oh – er – when all this happened.'

'How did you hear? Telephone or telegram[9]?'

'Telegram.'

'When was it sent?'

'I – I don't know exactly.'

'When did you receive it?'

'I was staying at Danebury Head so somebody phoned to tell me about it.'

'Danebury Head is quite near here, isn't it?'

'Yes. I got the message when I came in from playing golf and then I immediately came here.'

Miss Marple looked at him. He looked hot. She said: 'I've heard it's very pleasant at Danebury Head, and not very expensive.'

'No, I couldn't afford it if it was expensive. It's a nice little place. Right, I'd better get some exercise before lunch.' He walked away.

'Does he seem rather boring to you?' asked Sir Henry.

'Perhaps,' said Miss Marple.

Sir Henry stood up.

'Ah, here comes Mrs Bantry. She's arrived just at the right moment, as I must go and see Edwards.'

CHAPTER 13

In a quiet hotel room, Edwards said to Sir Henry Clithering:

'I understand you, sir. You want me to speak honestly – to say things that I usually shouldn't say.

'Of course I know Mr Jefferson well. He's a nice man, but I've seen him become <u>violent</u> with anger. The thing he hates most is people lying to him… In my opinion, sir, Ruby Keene didn't care about Mr Jefferson and she wasn't the girl Mr Jefferson thought she was. It was strange, how much he liked her. But young Mrs Jefferson changed this summer and it upset him. He's fond of her, you see. He's never liked Mr Mark much.'

'What do you think Mr Jefferson would do if Mark married someone else?' asked Sir Henry.

'Oh, Mr Jefferson would be very angry.'

'And if Mrs Jefferson married again?'

'He definitely wouldn't like that either, sir.'

'Do you remember any time when Mr Jefferson discussed his plans about Ruby with his family?'

'There was very little discussion, sir. Mr Jefferson just told them what he was planning to do. Mr Mark didn't like it. Mrs Jefferson didn't say much, only asked him not to do anything in a hurry.'

'And what about Ruby? Do you think she was a gold-digger?'

It was immediately clear from Edwards' face that he hadn't liked Ruby. 'Well, she was young, but she was learning quickly. She acted as if she had won something.'

'And did you think that maybe she had another special male friend?'

Edwards said slowly: 'There *was* something, sir. One day Miss Keene opened her handbag and a small photo fell out. Mr Jefferson picked it up and said: "Who's this?"'

'It was a photo of a young man, sir. Miss Keene pretended that she didn't know anything about it. She said: "I've no idea, Jeffie. I don't know how it could have got into my bag. *I* didn't put it there!"'

'He looked angry and said: "Now, Ruby. *You* know who it is – tell me."'

'She looked frightened and said: "Oh, I recognize him now. He comes here sometimes and I've danced with him. I don't know his name. He must have put his photo into my bag one day. These boys are so silly!"'

'I don't think Mr Jefferson believed her. After that, if she'd been out, he asked her where she'd been.'

In the police station at Danemouth, Superintendent Harper was interviewing five Girl Guides.

Pamela Reeves had told them only that she was going to Woolworth's and would get a later bus home.

In the corner of Superintendent Harper's office sat an elderly lady. The girls thought that she was also there to be interviewed.

When the girls had gone, Superintendent Harper looked at Miss Marple.

She spoke quickly. 'I'd like to speak to Florence.'

The girl was brought back in. She was tall, with blonde hair and frightened brown eyes.

Superintendent Harper stood up. 'This lady is going to ask you some more questions,' he said, and he left the room.

Miss Marple said: 'Sit down, Florence.'

Florence sat down next to Miss Marple. She suddenly felt less scared.

Miss Marple said:

'Florence, do you understand that it's very important that the police know everything that poor Pamela did on the day she died? If you don't tell them something that you know, that is a crime.

'I know that you're afraid. You probably think that people will be angry with you for not telling them everything earlier. But you've got to be brave and tell me now! Pamela wasn't going to Woolworth's. She was meeting someone about a film, wasn't she?' asked Miss Marple.

Florence looked relieved.

'Oh, *yes!*' she said quickly. 'Oh, I've been so worried. I promised Pam I'd never tell anyone. It's my fault she died. I should have stopped her.'

'Tell me what happened.'

'She met an important film director a while ago, from Lemville Studios. He told Pam that he was looking for a girl to be in his new film. He said that Pam would be perfect, but she had to have a test in front of the camera.

'So Pam was going to meet him at his hotel after the Guides. Then she could catch the bus home. He told her to tell her parents that she'd been shopping.'

Florence began to cry. 'I should have stopped her. I should have known that things like that don't really happen. I should have told someone. Oh, I wish I was *dead!*'

Five minutes later, Miss Marple was telling the story to Superintendent Harper.

'The clever man!' he said. 'But you aren't surprised, are you?'

'No, I expected something like this.'

'How did you know that that girl knew something? I thought she looked exactly the same as the others.'

Miss Marple said gently:

'You haven't had as much experience with girls telling lies as I have. Florence looked straight at you when you were speaking, just like the other girls did. But you didn't watch her as she went out of the door. I knew then that she'd got something to hide. People always relax too soon when they are hiding something. My maid Janet used to tell me that the mice had eaten the cake and then she always smiled as she left the room. So I knew it was her who'd eaten the cake.'

Miss Marple stood up.

'I must hurry back to the hotel to pack.' she said. 'I'm going back to St Mary Mead – there's a lot for me to do there.'

CHAPTER 14

Back in St Mary Mead, Miss Marple walked quickly up to the door of Basil Blake's cottage. She had a small black book in her hand. She knocked at the door, which was opened by Dinah Lee – the young blonde woman. She was wearing less make-up than usual.

'Good morning,' said Miss Marple in a cheerful voice. 'May I come in for a minute?'

She moved forward as she spoke, so that Dinah had no time to say no.

'Thank you so much,' said Miss Marple, sitting down on a chair. 'I just called to ask you to give some money to our local charity. Just a small amount?' Miss Marple held out her little book.

'Oh, well, I'm sure I can give you something.'

The girl turned to look for her handbag.

Miss Marple was looking round the room.

'I see you haven't got a rug in front of the fire.'

Dinah Lee turned round in surprise.

'There used to be one. I don't know where it's gone.'

'I suppose it was <u>fluffy</u>, was it?' asked Miss Marple.

'Yes, it was,' said Dinah, while thinking to herself, 'What a strange old lady!'

She held out some money.

'Here you are.'

'Oh, thank you. What name shall I write down?'

Dinah wasn't happy. '<u>Nosey</u> old cat,' she thought.

'Miss Dinah Lee,' she replied, smiling politely.

Miss Marple looked at her.

'This is Mr Basil Blake's cottage, isn't it?'

'Yes, and I'm *Miss* Dinah Lee!' Dinah replied.

Very slowly and seriously, Miss Marple said: 'I want to advise you, very strongly, to *stop* using your <u>maiden name</u> in St Mary Mead. Very soon you may need all the support you can get. I'm sure it has been very funny for you both to pretend that you are not married, but as you know, people who live in the country do not like people living together who are not married.'

Dinah looked shocked. 'How – how did you know we're married? Did you go to Somerset House[10]?' she demanded.

Miss Marple shook her head. 'Oh, it was quite easy to *guess*. Everybody talks about everything in a village and the – er – the kind of arguments you and Mr Blake have are typical of the early days of marriage – not at all like the arguments people who are not married have. People say that you can only really make someone upset if you are married to them. I've noticed that married people often enjoy their battles.'

She paused.

'Well, I—' Dinah stopped and laughed. 'You're absolutely marvellous! But why do you want us to admit that we're married?'

'Because, any minute now *your husband may be arrested for murder.*'

Dinah was shocked.

'You mean that girl at the Majestic Hotel? Do they think *Basil* killed her?'

'Yes.'

There was the sound of a car outside. Basil Blake came in, carrying some bottles. He said:

'I've got the drinks. Did you—?'

He stopped when he saw the visitor.

Dinah said: 'Is she mad? She says you're going to be arrested for the murder of that girl, Ruby Keene.'

'Oh, no!' said Basil Blake. The bottles dropped from his arms onto the sofa. He dropped down into a chair and put his face in his hands. 'Oh, no! Oh, no!'

Dinah went to him. 'Basil, I don't believe it for a moment!'

He took her hand.

'Thank you.'

'But why do they think—? You didn't even *know* her, did you?'

'Oh, yes, he knew her,' said Miss Marple.

'Be quiet!' Basil shouted. 'Dinah, I just saw her once or twice at the Majestic. That's all.'

'Why should anyone suspect you, then?'

Miss Marple said:

'What did you do with the rug?'

'I put it in the bin.'

Miss Marple said:

'It was fluffy, so the sparkles from her dress got caught in it, did they?'

'Yes, I couldn't get them out.'

Dinah cried: 'What are you both talking about?'

'I'll tell you what I think happened,' said Miss Marple. 'You can tell me if I'm not correct, Mr Blake. I think that you had an argument with your wife at a party, so you drove home without her. I don't know what time you arrived—'

'About two in the morning. I opened the door and turned on the light and I saw— I saw—'

He stopped.

'You saw a girl lying on the rug, in a white evening dress, strangled. Did you recognize her?'

Basil Blake shook his head.

'Oh no, I couldn't look at her! And Dinah was going to arrive home and find me here with a body and she'd think I killed her.

Then I had an idea – it seemed good at the time. I thought: "I'll put her in Bantry's library. He's a horrible old man – he thinks there's something wrong with me because I work in films. He'll look like a fool when a dead girl is found on his rug."

'By the morning I realized what a stupid thing I'd done. Then the police came here. I was scared, so I hid it by being rude to them. In the middle of it all Dinah came home.'

Dinah looked out of the window.

'There's a car driving up now...'

'It's the police, I think,' said Miss Marple.

Basil stood up. He was suddenly calm.

'So they're going to arrest me? All right – Dinah, call Mr Sims – he's the family lawyer. Then go to Mother and tell her we're married – she'll help us. And don't worry. *I didn't do it.* So it's going to be all right.'

There was a knock on the cottage door. Basil called 'Come in.' Inspector Slack entered with another man.

'Mr Basil Blake? I'm here to arrest you...'

Then the Inspector saw Miss Marple: 'Good morning,' he said and thought to himself:

'Smart old cat, she knew he did it! It's lucky we found his rug. And we know from the car-park man that he left that party at *eleven*, not at midnight. We've got him!'

When they were alone, Dinah Blake said to Miss Marple: 'I don't know who you are, but I believe Basil – *he didn't do it.*'

'Yes, I know he didn't – and I know who *did*. But it isn't going to be easy to prove. I think that something you said just now might help. It gave me an idea about the *connection* I've been trying to find. Now what *was* it?'

CHAPTER 15

Mrs Bantry hurried to the front door, opened it quickly, and greeted Miss Marple with a very worried look on her face.

'I've been calling *everywhere* looking for you. People are beginning to avoid Arthur. We *must* do something, Jane!'

Colonel Bantry appeared.

'Ah, Miss Marple. Good morning. I'm glad you've come. My wife's been ringing you like a mad woman.'

Miss Marple smiled.

'I wanted to bring you the news myself,' she said. 'Basil Blake has just been arrested for the murder of Ruby Keene.'

'Oh!' Mrs Bantry was surprised. 'Are you saying that he strangled that girl and then brought her here and put her in *our* library?'

'He put her in your library, but he didn't kill her. He found her dead in his cottage.'

'Oh, I don't believe that,' said the Colonel. 'If you find a body, you ring the police – if you're an honest man.'

'Ah,' said Miss Marple, 'but we're not all as calm and sensible as you are, Colonel Bantry. Young people are different. Some of them have had a difficult time. Did you know that Basil did ARP work[11] when he was only eighteen? He went into a burning house and brought out four children. Then he went back in for their dog, although they told him it wasn't safe. The building fell on him. They got him out, but he was in hospital for nearly a year and was ill for a long time after that. That's when he became interested in films.'

'Oh! I – I never knew that,' said the Colonel quietly.

'He doesn't talk about it,' said Miss Marple.

'He's a stronger man than I thought,' continued Colonel Bantry. 'I always thought he'd avoided the war, you know.'

Colonel Bantry looked ashamed.

'But why did he try to make it look as if *I* was the murderer?'

'I think he thought it was a joke.'

'Oh, I see.' He looked at Miss Marple. 'But *you* don't think he murdered her? And you think you know who did?'

Miss Marple nodded her head.

Mrs Bantry said happily to her husband: 'Isn't she wonderful?'

'Well, who was it?' continued the Colonel.

Miss Marple said: 'I need the Superintendent's help before I can tell you that…'

Chapter 16

It was three o'clock in the morning. The wind was quiet and the moon was shining over the calm sea.

In Conway Jefferson's room there was no sound except his own breathing.

There was no breeze to move the curtains at the window, but they moved... For a moment they opened and a person stood there.

Nearer and nearer to the bed that person came, with a hypodermic needle ready in their hand.

And then suddenly, out of the shadows, another hand grabbed the one that held the needle.

The voice of the law said: 'No, you don't. I'll take that needle!'

The light came on, and from his bed Conway Jefferson looked at the murderer of Ruby Keene.

CHAPTER 17

'I want to know how you do it, Miss Marple,' Sir Henry Clithering said.

Miss Marple smiled. 'I'm afraid that most people – including many policemen – believe what they are told. I never do.

'In this case,' she continued, 'certain things were <u>taken for granted</u> from the beginning. When I saw the body, I saw that the *facts* were that the victim was quite young, that she bit her nails and that her teeth stuck out a little.

'Of course, it was very confusing that she was found in Colonel Bantry's library. The murderer's plan was to put the body in poor Basil Blake's house and make *him* look like the murderer. I'm sure it must have annoyed the *real* murderer that Mr Blake moved the body to the Colonel's library.

'If the murderer's plan had worked, Mr Blake would have been the first person the police suspected. They would have made inquiries at Danemouth and discovered that he knew the girl. They'd think that Ruby asked him for money to keep quiet about their relationship, or something like that, and that he'd got angry, lost control and strangled her.

'But that all went wrong when Mr Blake moved the body, and the police started to look closely at the Jefferson family instead.

'I thought immediately about *money*. Two people would benefit from this girl's death – Mrs Jefferson and Mr Gaskell. Fifty thousand pounds is a lot of money, especially when you have financial problems. So money was the obvious motive. Of course they both seemed like very nice people, but you can never be sure, can you?

'Everyone liked Mrs Jefferson. But she was tired of her life and she was worried about her son's future; and some women have the strange idea that crimes they do for their children are almost <u>justified</u>.

'Mr Gaskell was a much more likely murderer. But, for a few reasons, I believed that a *woman* was involved in this crime.

'It was annoying, therefore, to find that both these people who had motives, also had alibis for the time when Ruby Keene died.

'But then there was the burnt-out car with Pamela Reeves's body in it. I now had two *halves* of the case, but they did not match. The one person who I *knew* was involved in the crime – Basil Blake – didn't have a motive.

'Then Dinah Lee mentioned something that I might never have thought of – the most obvious thing in the world. Somerset House! Marriage! If either Mr Gaskell or Mrs Jefferson was married, or even were *going* to get married, *then the wife or husband was probably involved too*. Raymond Starr, for example, might want to marry a rich wife. I think it was him who made Adelaide decide that she didn't want to be a widow anymore.

'As well as Raymond, there was Mr McLean. *He* wasn't rich either, and he *was* nearby on the night of the murder.

'So it began to seem as though *anyone* might have done it!

'But really, in my mind, I *knew*. It was all about those bitten nails...'

'Nails?' said Sir Henry. 'But Ruby broke her nail and cut the others.'

'Perhaps, but it isn't that simple. *Bitten* nails and short, *cut* nails are quite different! Those nails could only mean one thing – *the body in the library wasn't Ruby Keene!*

'And that brings us straight to the one person who *must* be involved. *Josie!* Josie saw the body. She *must* have known that it wasn't Ruby. So why did she tell us that it was?

'She also couldn't understand why the body was at Gossington Hall. Why? Because *she* knew where it should have been found! In Basil Blake's cottage.

'She made us think about Basil, too, by saying to Raymond that Ruby might have been with the film man. And she also put a photo of Basil into Ruby's handbag.

'On top of all that, she was angry. She was so angry with the dead girl that she couldn't hide it, even when she looked down at her dead body.

'That is what I meant about policemen believing what they're told. Nobody thought that Josie was lying when she said that the body was Ruby Keene's – why would she lie? So I knew that Josie was involved, but why would she want Ruby dead? Then, when Dinah Lee mentioned Somerset House, I finally understood the connection.

'Mark Gaskell and Josie got married a year ago. They knew that Mr Jefferson would change his will when he found out, so they decided to keep it a secret until he died. But they needed that to happen quickly, so they made a plan.

'It was really a very interesting plan. First of all, they chose the poor child, Pamela. They offered her a test for a film! She couldn't say no when Mark Gaskell offered it to her. He takes her in to the hotel by the side door and introduces her to Josie – he tells her she's one of their make-up experts – Josie dyes Pamela's hair, puts make-up on her and paints her fingernails. During all this, they give her a sweet drink that is drugged, and she falls asleep.

'After dinner Mark Gaskell went out in his car. That's when he took Pamela to Basil's cottage, still asleep and dressed in one of Ruby's old dresses, and strangled her... Oh, explaining this, I feel quite pleased to think of Mr Gaskell being hanged[12]!

'Then he drove back to the hotel and found the others. Ruby Keene was dancing with Raymond.

'Pamela's body was so important because it would confuse the police – they would think that Ruby had died at a time when both Mark and Josie had strong alibis. But at that time, Ruby was actually still alive.

'I think that Josie had given Ruby instructions – Ruby always did what Josie told her. She asked her to change her dress, go into Josie's room, and wait. They drugged her too, probably in her coffee after dinner. She seemed tired, remember, when she danced with Mr Bartlett.

'Josie came up later to "look for her" with Raymond – *but only Josie went into Josie's room when she had to change her dress to dance with Raymond.* She probably killed Ruby then.

'Then she went downstairs, danced with Raymond, talked about where Ruby could be with the Jeffersons, and finally went to bed. In the early hours of the morning, she dressed the girl in Pamela's clothes, carried the body down the side stairs, drove two miles in George Bartlett's car, poured petrol over the car and set fire to it. Then she walked back to the hotel.

'She was very clever,' said Miss Marple. 'She even thought about the nails – that Pamela's nails would be shorter than Ruby's. That's why she managed to break one of Ruby's nails on her scarf. It made an excuse for pretending that Ruby had cut her nails short.'

Harper said: 'And the only real evidence you had, Miss Marple, was a schoolgirl's bitten nails.'

'More than that,' said Miss Marple. 'People *do* talk too much. Mark Gaskell did. He was talking about Ruby and he said "her teeth went in." But the dead girl in Colonel Bantry's library had teeth that stuck *out*.'

Conway Jefferson said rather seriously:

'And was the way it ended so dramatically in my room your idea, Miss Marple?'

'Yes, it was. You see, once Mark and Josie knew that you were going to make a new will, they'd *have* to do something. I asked Superintendent Harper to ask you to tell them that you were going to make a new will the next day and leave all your money to charity. We knew that they would have to do something that night. The Superintendent then organised for some police officers to enter your bedroom without anyone seeing them.

'Mark knew that he was already a suspect, so he went off to London and had dinner at a restaurant with friends. Josie was going to do it. In the needle was something that would make it look like Mr Jefferson's heart had stopped by itself – any doctor would think that the death was quite natural. I think Josie was going to throw a big stone off the balcony afterwards. People would think that he died because of the shock of the noise.'

Sir Henry said: 'So the third death you spoke of was to be Conway Jefferson?'

Miss Marple shook her head.

'Oh no, I meant Basil Blake. They'd have got him hanged if they could.'

Conway Jefferson said.

'I always knew Rosamund had married a bad man. Well, he and Josie will both hang now.'

Miss Marple said: 'Josie was always the strong character – it was her plan. The <u>irony</u> of it is that she asked Ruby to come to the Majestic Hotel – she never thought that Mr Jefferson would like her so much that Ruby would ruin all her own plans to get his money.'

Jefferson said: 'Poor little Ruby...'

At that moment, Adelaide Jefferson and Hugo McLean came in. Adelaide looked almost beautiful tonight. She walked over to Conway Jefferson, put a hand on his shoulder, and said:

'I want to tell you something, Jeff. I'm going to marry Hugo.'

Conway Jefferson said: 'It's time you married again. Congratulations to you both. By the way, Addie, I'm making a new will tomorrow. I'm giving you ten thousand pounds and everything else I have goes to Peter when I die.'

'Oh, *Jeff*!' She started to cry. 'You're *wonderful*!'

'He's a nice boy. I'd like to see him a lot... in the time I've got left.'

'Oh, you will!'

Later, Hugo and Adelaide met Raymond downstairs.

Adelaide said, quickly:

'I must tell you my news. Hugo and I are getting married.'

The smile on Raymond's face was brave and perfect.

He looked into her eyes. 'I hope that you will be very, very happy.'

Raymond watched the couple as they walked away.

'She's a nice woman,' he said to himself. 'And with her I would have had money too. And I went to so much effort to pretend I was a Devonshire Starr... Oh well, better luck next time. Dance, dance, little man!'

✦ Character list ✦

Colonel Arthur Bantry: owner of Gossington Hall

Mrs Dolly Bantry: wife of Colonel Bantry of Gossington Hall; friend of Miss Jane Marple

Mary: maid at Gossington Hall

Lorrimer: butler at Gossington Hall

Miss Jane Marple: elderly unmarried lady with a reputation for solving murder mysteries; friend of Dolly Bantry's

Constable Palk: village policeman

Colonel Melchett: Chief Constable of the Radfordshire police, and a friend of the Bantrys'

Inspector Slack: a police detective who works for Colonel Melchett

Basil Blake: a young man who works in the film industry

Dinah Lee: a young woman who lives with Blake

Dr Haydock: local GP and police doctor

Ruby Keene: eighteen-year-old professional dancer who works at the Majestic Hotel

Josie Turner: a dancer and bridge hostess who also works at the Majestic Hotel; Ruby's cousin

Raymond Starr: professional dancer and tennis teacher who also works at the Majestic Hotel

Conway Jefferson: a rich elderly businessman staying at the Majestic Hotel

Mark Gaskell: Conway Jefferson's son-in-law also staying at the Majestic Hotel

Adelaide Jefferson: Conway Jefferson's daughter-in-law, also staying at the Majestic Hotel

Peter Carmody: nine-year-old son from Adelaide's first marriage, also staying at the Majestic Hotel

George Bartlett: young man staying at the Majestic Hotel

Mr Prestcott: manager of the Majestic Hotel

Superintendent Harper: a detective with the Glenshire Police

Sir Henry Clithering: retired head of the London Police, and friend of Conway Jefferson's

Hugo McLean: a friend of Adelaide's

Pamela Reeves: a sixteen-year-old Girl Guide

Dr Metcalf: a doctor

Edwards: Conway Jefferson's driver and helper

Florence Small: Girl Guide and friend of Pamela's

◆ CULTURAL NOTES ◆

1. The British class system

In 1942, when *The Body in the Library* was written, Britain had a class system with rules that everybody knew and most people followed. Some of the *upper class* had titles like Duke, Marquess and Sir, but many were just families who had owned large estates for centuries and often had no titles. *Colonel Bantry* and *Colonel Melchett* belong to this group. Their titles are military titles awarded to members of the upper classes. *Raymond Starr* says he is from an upper-class family, the Starrs, who live in Devonshire, in the south-west of England, but who have lost all their money.

The *middle classes* were educated people who had to work for a living – in the law, medicine, education, business, the Church or something similar.

The *working classes* were educated as far as they legally had to be – at that time you could leave school when you were fourteen – and were generally involved in all other work not done by the middle and upper classes. Many were employed in the houses of wealthy families, like *Mary*, the Bantrys' maid, and *Lorrimer*, their butler. In *The Body in the Library* it is obvious to the characters that *Ruby Keene* is from a lower class.

This class system lasted until the Second World War (1939-1945) when many social rules changed, especially the role of women in society.

2. Country houses

Rich people often had large houses with gardens and farm land in the country and lived comfortable lives with a lot of free time for social activities and running the local area. Gossington Hall in this story is one of those houses. These houses had servants who lived and worked there. Servants looked after the family's clothes, and did the cleaning and cooking. The larger the house, the more servants there were.

Servants in these houses had their own class system, with different jobs for men and women. The butler was the main male servant, and was in charge. The housekeeper was the main female servant. She was in charge of the maids (the women who cleaned the house and looked after the family's clothes) and was the main contact with the mistress of the house. The cook was in charge of the food. A valet looked after the master's clothes and a lady's maid would do the lady of the house's hair. There would also be many gardeners.

Servants worked long hours for little money, and often worked in the same house all their lives. They knew a lot about the family who lived in the house, but it was considered wrong to talk about them to outsiders.

In this story the *Bantrys* are rich – they have a maid, a butler, a cook and a driver.

3. Village life
An English village is a small group of houses in the countryside, usually with a church at its centre. Sometimes there is a very large house in or near a village where upper class people live. They may own the local farmland and the houses of farm workers. In the days when this book was written, a village often had a post office, an inn (or pub), and a few shops. It might also have had a local doctor.

Historically, village life was quieter and slower than life in a town and everyone knew who everyone else was, even if they did not meet socially. They also knew quite a lot about each other's lives.

Village life was very traditional and conservative. Few people had cars, so ordinary village people led quite isolated lives. The train was the only means of long distance transport for most people.

4. The structure of the police in England

The Metropolitan Police was created in London in 1829. The ranks, starting at the lowest, are Police Constable, Sergeant, Inspector, Chief Inspector, Superintendent, Chief Superintendent and then Commissioner. The Commissioner is the highest-ranking police officer in the United Kingdom. So in *The Body in the Library*, *Sir Henry Clithering* was once the highest police officer in the UK. He no longer works because he is too old.

Each English county has its own police force. Each one has a Chief Constable in charge. The Chief Constable does not usually participate in investigations – he is a manager who makes important decisions. In this story, however, the Chief Constable, *Colonel Melchett*, becomes involved because he is a friend of *Colonel Bantry*.

Police forces from different counties work together when a case affects both counties.

5. Bridge

This is one of the world's most popular card games. It is played by four players in two pairs. Partners sit opposite each other around a table.

6. Wills

A will is an important document. It describes how somebody's money and possessions are to be divided between family and others when that person dies. In 1942, when *The Body in the Library* was written, if a person did not make a will, everything went to the oldest son. This meant that most women of the middle and upper classes (who usually did not work) needed their husband, father or brother to write a will or they would have no money to live on after their deaths. A person can change their will at any time, but it must be signed by another person to show that it is a real will.

7. The story of King Cophetua and the maid

This is the story of a young African king, Cophetua, who could have married any of the princesses he met, but he thought they were all boring. Instead, he chose to marry a poor young girl who he found on the streets selling wild flowers.

8. Public-school education

In the UK, public schools are very expensive independent schools. Many of Britain's prime ministers, politicians, judges and top army people have been educated at a public school. However, *Raymond Starr* says that it is because he went to such a good school that he can't get a 'normal' job, because people who go to public schools do not usually do 'normal' jobs, because they are upper class (see cultural note 1). This also suggests that Raymond is not very intelligent and did not do very well academically at school.

9. Telegram

In 1942, when *The Body in the Library* was written, one of the main forms of long-distance communication was by telegram. A telegram was a message sent through a telegraph machine using electricity or radio signals. The message was then printed and delivered to someone's home. The messages had to be very short.

10. Somerset House

In 1942, when *The Body in the Library* was written, all British public records, such as birth certificates and marriage certificates were kept at Somerset House in central London. Anybody could visit to look at the certificates which is why *Dinah Lee* asks *Miss Marple* if she has been there and checked her and *Basil Blake*'s certificate.

11. ARP

In 1937, the British government created the Air Raid Wardens' Service. The Service was to protect people from air raids if there was a war. An air raid was when enemy planes flew over the country and dropped bombs on towns and cities. The volunteers who worked in the Service were called ARP wardens. When the Second World War started in 1939, ARP wardens walked the streets at night and made sure you couldn't see any lights from houses or other buildings. If there were lights, it helped the enemy bomber planes to see where the towns and cities were. When planes were flying over the town or city, ARP wardens would try and get people into the underground shelters for safety. ARP wardens were usually part-time volunteers who had full-time day jobs, so it was tiring work, and very dangerous – almost 7,000 ARP wardens were killed doing it.

12. The death penalty

When *The Body in the Library* was first published in 1942, anyone who killed a person on purpose could be hanged by the neck. Hanging meant they tied a rope around the person's neck and then dropped them through an automatic door. Hanging by the rope, they could not breathe and died. This was called the death penalty. The death penalty for murder ended in the UK in 1965.

⬦ Glossary ⬦

adopt TRANSITIVE VERB
If you **adopt** someone else's child, you take it into your own family and make it legally yours.

alibi COUNTABLE NOUN
If you have an **alibi**, you can prove that you were somewhere else when a crime took place.

amateur ADJECTIVE
Amateur activities are done by people as a hobby and not as a job.

ambitious ADJECTIVE
Someone who is **ambitious** wants to be successful, rich, or powerful.

as far as I know PHRASE
You use 'as far as I know' to show that you are not absolutely sure of what you are about to say or have just said, and you may be wrong.

bend down PHRASAL VERB
When you **bend down**, you move the top part of your body down and forwards.

benefit INTRANSITIVE VERB
If you **benefit** from something, it helps you or improves your life.

burglar COUNTABLE NOUN
A **burglar** is a thief who breaks into houses and steals things.

burnt-out ADJECTIVE
Burnt-out vehicles or buildings have been very badly damaged by fire.

busybody COUNTABLE NOUN
If you say that someone is a **busybody**, you dislike the way that they are interested in what other people are doing.

calm (down) TRANSITIVE VERB
If you **calm** someone, or if you **calm** them **down**, you do something to make them less upset or excited.

case COUNTABLE NOUN
A **case** is a crime that the police are working on.

clipping COUNTABLE NOUN
Fingernail or nail **clippings** are
small pieces of nail that have
been cut off from longer nails.

clue COUNTABLE NOUN
A **clue** to a problem or mystery is
something that helps you find the
answer.

cold ADJECTIVE
A **cold** person does not show
much emotion or affection and
therefore seems unfriendly.

Colonel TITLE NOUN
Colonel is a senior position in
the army, navy or air force.

connection COUNTABLE NOUN
A **connection** is a relationship
between two people, groups, or
things.

county COUNTABLE NOUN
A **county** is a region of Britain,
Ireland, or the USA with its own
local government.

crude ADJECTIVE
Something that is **crude** is simple
and not sophisticated.

curiosity UNCOUNTABLE NOUN
Curiosity is wanting to know
about things.

deliberately ADVERB
If you do something **deliberately**,
you intend to do it.

devoted ADJECTIVE
If you are **devoted** to someone or
something, you care about them
or love them very much.

dramatically ADVERB
If someone does something
dramatically, they do it in an
excited way.

dressing gown COUNTABLE NOUN
A **dressing gown** is a loose coat
worn over pyjamas or other night
clothes.

drug TRANSITIVE VERB
If you **drug** a person, you give
them a pill or a drink in order to
make them sleepy.

dyed ADJECTIVE
If something such as hair or
clothes are **dyed**, the colour is
changed by putting them in a
special liquid.

evidence UNCOUNTABLE NOUN
Evidence is information which is used to prove that something is true.

examination COUNTABLE NOUN
If someone gives something an **examination**, they look at it carefully.

favour TRANSITIVE VERB
If you **favour** someone, you are nicer to them than you are to other people.

finances PLURAL NOUN
Your **finances** are the amount of money that you have.

(finger)nail COUNTABLE NOUN
Your **fingernails** or your **nails** are the hard areas on the ends of your fingers.

fingerprint COUNTABLE NOUN
Your **fingerprints** are the marks made by your fingers when you touch something.

fluffy ADJECTIVE
Something such as a towel or rug that is **fluffy** is very soft.

fool TRANSITIVE VERB
If someone **fools** you, they make you believe something that is not true.

there's no fool like an old fool PHRASE
The expression '**there's no fool like an old fool**' is used to say that a foolish old person is especially foolish because an old person should be more sensible than a young person.

frown INTRANSITIVE VERB
If you **frown**, you move your eyebrows close together because you are annoyed, worried, or thinking hard.

get on with PHRASAL VERB
If you **get on with** an activity, you continue doing it or start doing it.

Girl Guides PROPER NOUN
In Britain (and many other countries), a **Girl Guide** is a girl who is a member of an organization which teaches girls to look after themselves.

give in PHRASAL VERB
If you **give in**, you agree to do something that you do not want to do.

gold-digger COUNTABLE NOUN
A **gold-digger** is a person who has a relationship with someone who is rich in order to get money or expensive things from them.

grief-stricken ADJECTIVE
If someone is **grief-stricken**, they are very sad about something that has happened.

grip TRANSITIVE VERB
If you **grip** something, you hold it tightly.

grunt INTRANSITIVE VERB
If someone **grunts**, they make a low noise, often because they do not want to talk.

harm UNCOUNTABLE NOUN
To cause someone **harm** means to injure them.

healer COUNTABLE NOUN
A **healer** is a person or thing which makes people feel better.

hostess COUNTABLE NOUN
A **hostess** is a woman who looks after and entertains the guests at a club.

hypodermic needle COUNTABLE NOUN
A **hypodermic needle** is used to give injections of medicine.

-in-law SUFFIX
-in-law is used to talk about the parents and close relatives of your husband or wife. For example, your **father-in-law** is the father of your husband or wife.

innocent ADJECTIVE
If someone is **innocent**, they did not do a crime which other people said they did.

invalid COUNTABLE NOUN
An **invalid** is someone who is very ill or who has a disability and needs to be cared for by someone else.

investigate TRANSITIVE VERB
If someone, **investigates** an event or a crime, they try to find out what happened or what is the truth.

irony VARIABLE NOUN
The **irony** of a situation is an aspect of it which is strange or amusing, because it is the opposite of what you expect.

justified ADJECTIVE
A decision, action, or idea that is **justified** has been shown to be sensible or necessary.

kill two birds with one stone PHRASE
If you say that doing something will **kill two birds with one stone**, you mean that it will let you do two things that you want to do, rather than just one.

knowledge UNCOUNTABLE NOUN
Knowledge is information and understanding about a subject, which someone has in their mind.

library COUNTABLE NOUN
In some large houses the **library** is the room where most of the books are kept.

limp COUNTABLE NOUN
If you walk with a **limp**, you do not walk very well because one of your legs or feet is hurt.

maiden name COUNTABLE NOUN
A married woman's **maiden name** is her surname before she got married.

mental ADJECTIVE
Mental means relating to the mind and the process of thinking.

misunderstanding VARIABLE NOUN
A **misunderstanding** is not understanding something such as a situation or what someone has said.

morals PLURAL NOUN
Morals are what you believe about what is right and wrong.

motive COUNTABLE NOUN
Your **motive** for doing something is your reason for doing it.

nail polish VARIABLE NOUN
Nail polish is a thick liquid that women paint on their nails.

nod INTRANSITIVE VERB
If you **nod**, you move your head down and up to show that you understand or like something, or that you agree with it.

nosey ADJECTIVE
If you describe someone as
nosey, you mean that they are
interested in what other people
are doing.

nothing to do with PHRASE
If something has **nothing to do
with** someone, it has no
connection to them.

overwhelmed ADJECTIVE
If you are **overwhelmed** by a
person, feeling or event, it has a
very strong effect on you and you
do not know how to deal with it.

physical ADJECTIVE
Physical means connected with a
person's body, rather than with
their mind.

plain ADJECTIVE
If you describe someone,
especially a woman or girl, as
plain, you think they look ordinary
and are not at all beautiful.

portrait COUNTABLE NOUN
A **portrait** is a painting, drawing,
or photograph of a person.

premeditated ADJECTIVE
A **premeditated** crime is planned
or thought about before it is done.

pretend TRANSITIVE VERB
If you **pretend** that something is
true, you try to make people
believe that it is true, although it
is not.

reaction VARIABLE NOUN
Your **reaction** to something that
has happened or something that
you have experienced is what you
feel, say, or do because of it.

registration number COUNTABLE
NOUN
The **registration number** of a car
is the group of letters and
numbers that are shown at the
front and back of it.

relieved ADJECTIVE
If you are **relieved**, you feel glad
because something unpleasant
has not happened or is no longer
happening.

ruin TRANSITIVE VERB
To **ruin** something means to harm,
damage, or spoil it completely.

sensitive ADJECTIVE
If you are **sensitive** about something, it worries or upsets you.

set alight PHRASE
If something has been **set alight**, it is burning.

set decorator COUNTABLE NOUN
A **set decorator** is in charge of getting furniture and other objects needed for making television programmes or films.

shake one's head PHRASE
If you **shake your head**, you move it from side to side in order to say 'no'.

shiver INTRANSITIVE VERB
When you **shiver**, your body shakes because you are cold or frightened.

shoelace COUNTABLE NOUN
Shoelaces are long, narrow pieces of material like pieces of string that you use to keep your shoes on.

Sir TITLE NOUN
Sir is the title used in front of the name of a knight or baronet. (*See also Cultural note 1*)

sparkle COUNTABLE NOUN
Sparkles are small, shiny circles that are sewn on clothes to decorate them.

specialized ADJECTIVE
Someone or something that is **specialized** is based around a particular area of knowledge.

stand guard PHRASE
When a soldier or police officer is **standing guard** at a place, they are watching it carefully.

startled ADJECTIVE
If you are **startled**, you are surprised and a little frightened.

statement COUNTABLE NOUN
A **statement** is a report that someone gives to the police about what happened.

stick out PHRASAL VERB
If something **sticks out**, you notice it more than something else.

strangle TRANSITIVE VERB
To **strangle** someone means to kill them by tightly squeezing their throat.

suspect COUNTABLE NOUN
A **suspect** is a person who the police think may be guilty of a crime.
TRANSITIVE VERB
If you **suspect** someone of doing something that is not honest or is unpleasant, you believe that they probably did it.

swollen ADJECTIVE
If a part of your body is **swollen**, it is larger and rounder than normal, usually as a result of injury or illness.

take something for granted PHRASE
If you **take something for granted**, you believe that it is true or you accept it as normal without thinking about it.

terrace COUNTABLE NOUN
A **terrace** is a flat area of stone or grass next to a building where people can sit.

tragedy VARIABLE NOUN
A **tragedy** is a very sad event or situation.

everything someone touches turns to gold PHRASE
If you say that **everything someone touches turns to gold**, you mean that they succeed easily at everything they do.

uncertainly ADVERB
If say or do something **uncertainly**, you do or say it but without being sure of what you are doing or saying.

victim COUNTABLE NOUN
A **victim** is someone who has been hurt or killed by someone or something.

violent ADJECTIVE
If someone is **violent**, they hurt or kill other people, sometimes using something like a gun or a knife.

the voice of the law PHRASE
If you talk about **the voice of the law**, you mean the police.

well educated ADJECTIVE
A **well educated** person has reached a high standard of learning.

well-used ADJECTIVE
If a place or object is described as **well-used**, it means it is probably dirty or spoiled because it has been used a lot.

widow COUNTABLE NOUN
A **widow** is a woman whose husband has died. A man whose wife has died is called a **widower**.

COLLINS ENGLISH READERS ONLINE

Go online to discover the following useful resources for teachers and students:

- Downloadable audio of the story

- Classroom activities, including a plot synopsis

- Student activities, suitable for class use or for self-studying learners

- A level checker to ensure you are reading at the correct level

- Information on the Collins COBUILD Grading Scheme

All this and more at **www.collinselt.com/readers**

COLLINS ENGLISH READERS

**Do you want to read more at your reading level?
Try these:**

AGATHA CHRISTIE MYSTERIES

Death on the Nile 978-0-00-824968-7
Murder on the Orient Express 978-0-00-824967-0
Dead Man's Folly 978-0-00-824970-0
The Witness for the Prosecution and Other Stories 978-0-00-824971-7

OTHER LEVEL 3 COLLINS ENGLISH READERS

Amazing Scientists 978-0-00-754510-0
Amazing Philanthropists 978-0-00-754504-9
Amazing Performers 978-0-00-754505-6
Amazing Explorers 978-0-00-754497-4
Amazing Writers 978-0-00-754498-1

Are you ready for Level 4? Use our online level checker to find out.

Find out more at **www.collinselt.com/readers**